A Burning Redemption

Ann S. Mooney

Numbers 6:24-26

Love,

Ann S. Mooney

I dedicate this book to my husband Sam. Your love and support gave me what I needed to write my dreams into stories that hold pieces of me in each character. Thank you for providing me with so much more than I could ever repay.

Contents

Colossians 2:6-8 KJV

As ye have therefore received Christ Jesus the Lord, so walk ye in Him: Rooted and built up in Him, and stablished in the faith, as ye have been taught, abounding therein with thanksgiving. Beware lest any man spoil you through philosophy and vain deceit, after the tradition of men, after the rudiments of the world, and not after Christ.

Chapter 1

Henry grunted as the stick jammed hard into his ribs.

"I told you not to do that. It's why I win every time." Christopher smirked darkly through piercing blue eyes.

"You don't know what you're doing any more than I do," Henry said as he threw down his stick, and glared at him as he pushed back his brown hair from his sweating face. "We need to find someone who can teach us for real."

"Well, I'm doing something right because you keep losing. I say we get Saul from down at the wharf to teach us." Christopher dropped his stick and stepped closer to Henry. He slicked his black hair back as he smirked. "You need more lessons than I do."

"I may not be able to beat you with swords, but I can throw a punch better than you." Henry retorted.

"So you say," Christopher smirked again and then suddenly popped his fist into Henry's ribs where he had struck him with his pretend sword.

Henry doubled over with a grimace.

"That was low to hit me where I'm wounded." Henry glared at Christopher again.

Christopher grinned, "Pirates don't play fair, so get used to it. Never let your guard down." He punched Henry's shoulder, "Even around your best friend."

Henry shook his head in annoyance, then turned his soft green eyes towards the bell in the church steeple that suddenly registered in his mind. The boys grimaced at each other before racing off toward the church. They reached it as the last of the townspeople were strolling into the building. Pastor Thomas

Johnson glared at the boys as they ran up.

"And where have you two been all morning?" he asked accusingly.

"Just out for a walk, Father," Henry lied politely.

"No doubt getting into trouble," his father said as he openly glared at Christopher. It was no secret the good pastor had no affection for Christopher. He blamed Christopher whenever there was trouble from the two boys. Usually pointing out that Christopher was just like his worthless father.

Christopher's drunken father was the reason so many townspeople looked down on him. Henry never judged Christopher like others. He was the only one Christopher trusted with the darkest parts of his life. Henry was the only one who knew Christopher went without food often or was the unwilling recipient of his father's drunken fist. Henry longed for the freedom Christopher had because no one cared what Christopher did. Henry's parents were loving Christian people who cared for their children but were strict in their expectations. Christopher secretly longed for what Henry had. A family that loved him.

"Get to your seat, son, and try to seek forgiveness for your lie." Henry's father held out a hand towards the door to indicate Henry should go in. Christopher followed quickly and sat in the back as Henry went to the front to sit with his mother and sister.

Henry sat down next to his sister Joanna, but his mind didn't focus on the sermon or anything else about the long service. His mind was full of dreams. Dreams of sailing on a ship full of pirates who could do anything they pleased. It was a dream he shared with Christopher, and they planned to leave when they were old enough, to seek their fortunes on the sea.

Henry found the service as boring as ever and was quick to take the opportunity to pull his mother aside, away from his father's listening ears, as soon as the service ended.

"Mother, may Christopher come for supper this evening?" he asked her quietly.

His kind mother had developed a soft spot for

Christopher since the day Henry had asked for extra food to take to school for Christopher. Ever since she always added extra food to his pail that he took for dinner at school, and she always said yes when he asked for his friend to come for supper.

"Yes, that will be alright I suppose," she said with a soft smile.

"Thank you, mother." Henry smiled and then left to find his friend outside by a tree. "Mother said you can come over tonight for supper."

Christopher stared at the ground. He was grateful for Henry's friendship but Henry's charity made him feel ashamed. He would try to do odd jobs on the wharf when ships came in, but it was hard for a boy his age to get work. Henry always seemed to know when he'd gone without food for a while. He didn't know how Henry knew but he was grateful to his friend. The only thing Christopher's father ever fed him was stale bread when he hadn't drunk the few coins he earned when sober enough to work.

Mrs. Johnson had become like a mother to Christopher, the only one he'd ever known. His mother died giving birth to him and his father never let him forget it. Usually with a slap to the face, a hard bruising punch to the arm, or a knock upside the head. A few times he locked Christopher in a closet for crying about being hungry when he was little. He hated his father and sometimes didn't go home when it was warm enough to sleep outside. Henry didn't know that part. He knew a lot but didn't know about Christopher sleeping outside to stay away from his father.

He had found a nice spot down by the river to sleep and bathe when he needed to. He even kept some clothes and a blanket there in case he couldn't go home. It had been a few days since he'd been home and he ran out of bread two days before. The weekends were the hardest because he didn't even have any food from Henry's dinners as he did on a school day. He was already hungry.

Christopher didn't care much about God since God hadn't

seen fit to help him in his life. He'd been caring for himself for as long as he could remember, and he saw no reason to start trusting someone who didn't care enough about him to feed him when he'd been hungry for days. He only went to church so Henry's family wouldn't stop inviting him over. It wasn't just about being hungry. Mrs. Johnson was warm-hearted and he was grateful to have her take him in the way she did. He didn't care much about pleasing anyone else, but she was the exception. She'd been good to him and he wanted her to know how grateful he was to her, so he agreed to go to church with them when she asked.

Pastor Johnson wasn't so keen on him, but Christopher didn't care much. The only people he cared for in this world were Mrs. Johnson and Henry.

"Chris?" Henry punched his arm and Christopher flinched.

"What?"

"Are you coming?" Henry asked with a frown.

"I'll be there. Thanks." Christopher walked away with his head held higher than he felt.

∞∞∞

"Joanna, please set the table." Mrs. Johnson instructed her daughter softly.

Joanna moved to do as she was told and gathered dishes to set the table.

"Set an extra place tonight," her mother said from the fireplace.

Joanna rolled her violet eyes and flung a piece of her raven-black hair behind her shoulder. She knew it. She knew her ridiculous brother had invited his trouble-making friend to supper. Her mother's weakness for Christopher annoyed her. She agreed with her father. He was nothing but trouble and had been a pain in her side since the day Henry had met him. He teased her whenever he was around, and it irritated her that a small part of her liked it.

Mary Beth and Susan constantly giggled behind their hands all day, every day at school. Whispering how they wished he would kiss them with his perfect lips. Johanna blushed as she set down a plate, knowing she couldn't help but agree with every other girl at school on that point. Then the thought of Mary Beth shamelessly flirting with him whenever she had the chance made her turn red in anger. Mary Beth would run her fingers through his thick black hair to lure him towards her to keep his bright blue eyes solely on her. Susan brought sweets from her father's store to share with him, and he gladly accepted them from her. Most of their efforts were put towards "helping" him with his schoolwork. He was the most handsome boy in town and he knew it. He knew the girls liked him and seemed to enjoy letting them do things for him. Otherwise, he seemed to not care about any of them. He just used them and then ignored them. He was no gentleman. Though she knew few boys who were. Most of the boys she knew were either rough or obnoxious. Christopher was both.

"I can't wait until Chris is done with school next year." Joanna grudgingly took another plate from the shelf as her mother stirred the pot of stew. She looked just like her mother and they were the subject of many of the curious gossips in town. She felt special and unique when people commented on how lovely her eyes were.

Christopher usually teased her, calling her Violet with a smirk. Part of her wished it was more lady-like to punch him for it. But there was a secret part of her that liked it just a little. He didn't tease any of the other girls at school. Only her. She started to smile to herself.

Joanna pinched herself. "Don't think like that. He doesn't deserve one ounce of your attention," she scolded herself.

"Talking about me, Violet?"

She froze and turned slightly to glare at him. He was grinning at her as Henry walked up behind Christopher.

"What?" Henry looked between them.

Christopher watched as Joanna stuck up her nose and walked back to the kitchen. He couldn't seem to shake the strange feeling that came over him whenever she was around. He couldn't seem to do anything but tease her and he didn't know why. He liked making her squirm, or stick up her nose. He admitted she was beautiful, but why should he care? Girls were only useful to a point. They were helpful and good at schoolwork, but he didn't believe they were worth his time. Most of them just seemed shallow to him. And yet, there was something about Joanna that felt different. She was mysterious and he always wanted to ask her what was behind her violet eyes. He might pay more attention to her if it wasn't for her father's hatred for him. Was any girl worth enduring her father's hatred?

He followed Henry to the table where they were met with the kind violet eyes of Mrs. Johnson. He smiled at her.

"Hello, Christopher," she said kindly.

"Thank you for having me, ma'am," he replied with genuine gratefulness.

"Am I right to assume the good smells mean it's time for supper, wife?" Pastor Johnson asked as he walked into the room. Then he saw Christopher and his face soured slightly. "Christopher."

"Sir." Christopher nodded slightly, "Thank you for having me. It's a blessing to be in your home, sir." Christopher may not care about God, but that didn't mean he didn't know what to say in the pastor's house.

The good pastor nodded slightly as he gestured for everyone to sit, and prayed for the food.

The meal was pleasant enough. Despite the pastor and Joanna's dislike for Christopher, they were used to having him around. When supper ended Henry dragged him to the sitting room for a game of chess. Chess was all about being cunning and having a strategy. Something he knew he should practice for his life as a pirate.

"Checkmate," Christopher said with a smirk.

Henry shook his head with a smile. "I let you win."

Christopher rolled his eyes, "Sure. Whatever you want to tell yourself." He stood and stretched. "I have to get going."

"Oh, come on, Chris. One more game." Henry said with a shake of his head.

"I can't. I gotta get going." Christopher walked over to Mrs. Johnson who was sitting on the settee bowed slightly. "Thank you for supper, ma'am. I appreciate your kindness."

She smiled at him, "You're very welcome, Christopher."

Then he turned to the pastor.

"Good evening, sir." Christopher nodded slightly.

"Good evening," the man said with just a glance at him.

Christopher turned to walk to the door and winked at Joanna as he passed her. He grinned when she stuck up her nose.

He made his way to his house near the wharf and snuck in as quietly as possible, but he missed seeing the empty bottle on the floor. He stepped on it and it rolled. He couldn't catch himself, falling with a loud thud, as the bottle loudly rolled away.

"What's…who's there? Is that you, you blockheaded boy?" His father's voice came from the bedroom and Christopher grimaced.

"Yes, sir," he stood and moved backward slowly as he listened to his father's footsteps coming out of the dark room.

"You woke me, boy!" the big man growled.

"Sorry, Pa," Christopher stopped as his back came against the wall and fear gripped him.

His father walked over and Christopher saw another bottle in his hand.

"Where you been, boy?" The big man stopped in front of him and looked down darkly.

"I was just out, Pa," Christopher winced at every movement his father made.

"You've been gone for days. Why come back now?" His father's voice rose with every sentence. "Why don't you just stay gone?! Then I won't have to look at you!"

Christopher closed his eyes before he felt the blow. The bottle hit him in the head with a painful thud and he crumpled to the floor.

When Christopher woke the next morning, his head pounded and his ribs hurt. His father must have kicked him for good measure. Christopher grimaced as he struggled to sit up. He should have waited till daylight to come home. At least his father wouldn't have been as drunk. Somehow his father managed to get enough work on the docks to pay for his bottles. Not a cent for his son. The most he'd ever given Christopher was bread and a beating. The only money Christopher saw came from the money he stole from his father, or what he could earn himself.

He stood up carefully and walked gingerly to the closet where he kept what little he had in the small house. He reached in and pulled out a semi-clean shirt. When he took off his blood stained-shirt, he looked down to see a nasty bruise over his ribs. He flinched as he touched it gingerly while putting on his shirt Then he left the house and walked towards the docks. Mr. Smith had promised him a job today and he didn't want to be late.

Christopher staggered into the warehouse, trying to ignore the looks he got from the other workers. He was sure there was probably a nasty cut on his head since there had been blood on his shirt.

"Mr. Smith, sir?"

Mr. Smith looked up and nodded. "Christopher, go find old Willy. He's in charge today."

Willy was nice enough. He was easy to talk to and told stories while they worked.

"Have you seen Saul lately?" Christopher asked Willy as they took inventory of a new load of crates off a ship.

"Why would you want to know about Saul? You know it's said he's a pirate." Willy looked at him with concern.

"That's just a rumor. I need his help with something is

all." Christopher shrugged like it was no big deal.

"I saw him working for Mr. Brown at the tavern. Though he might do more drinking than working there." Willy shook his head. "Stay away from him boy. He's no good."

Christopher didn't say any more. He couldn't help but feel like people thought the same thing about him. That he was no good, and not worth knowing.

"Well if that's the case then knowing Saul won't make it any worse," he thought.

When he finished with the work Mr. Smith had for him and got paid, he went to the tavern to find Saul. He entered the dingy building with a fireplace at one end of the rectangular room, and candles at each table. The tavern owner, Mr. Brown, was pouring drinks for different customers. Christopher sat down at a table and waited for the man to see him. When Mr. Brown walked over he frowned at the boy.

"Your pa was just here not an hour ago. Did he not get enough? I gave him two bottles."

Christopher grimaced. He would sleep by the river tonight for sure. Two bottles would last his father less than two nights. The stuff was strong and his father had a low tolerance for alcohol. He knew this because he'd seen other men drink just as much and not become drunken slobs.

"I'm looking for Saul, and I need supper," Christopher said with confidence.

"I'll have Saul bring you supper in a minute, but keep your business short. He's working off debt and I don't want him slacking off." Mr. Brown scowled and Christopher nodded.

Saul looked annoyed that he had to bring a young boy his supper. He almost plopped the plate in front of Christopher and sat down across the table.

"I hear you want to talk to me about something?" he said with a frown.

"Is it true you're a pirate?" Christopher asked quietly.

Saul looked at him with amusement.

"If I was, I wouldn't go around telling anyone. They hang

you for being that you know."

"I am looking for someone to teach me how to fight. I want to be a pirate and need to know how to use a sword." Christopher looked at Saul eagerly.

Saul looked at him like he was insane for a moment before he shrugged.

"If you work for Brown in my place then I will. I have a year's debt to pay off working for him. If you agree to help pay my debt, I will teach you to fight."

Christopher looked at him thoughtfully.

"I'll do it if you teach my friend too. And you'll teach us until I'm done helping you work off your debt."

Saul grinned suddenly, "Fine. The first lesson will be tomorrow. Eat up, because you have plates to wash."

Christopher dug in hungrily as his excitement grew. He couldn't wait to tell Henry their good fortune!

Chapter 2

"Go up," Christopher shouted.

Henry didn't listen though and the sword was knocked from his hand.

"I told you to go up," Christopher grumbled.

"I couldn't," Henry said tiredly.

"Alright, we have to get home." Joanna handed Christopher the sword. "Are you coming for supper tonight?"

"No, I have to be at the docks soon for a job." He looked at Henry, "Care to join us?"

"No, I've got to get home. I promised my father I'd do some work at the house for him." Henry handed Christopher his sword. "I'll see you tomorrow, Chris."

"Alright," Christopher said as he returned the swords to their hiding place.

Henry and Joanna turned and started for home. Henry had performed poorly at sparring today. He wished he were better with the sword. Saul had taught them many things in the year he had agreed to and Henry was grateful. They had been practicing for the last few years since they finished school while working odd jobs around the docks, taverns, or shops. Joanna had come upon them a couple of years ago and insisted they teach her as well. They weren't sure why she would want to learn sword and fighting skills. She wouldn't tell them, but they had agreed so she wouldn't tell their parents what they were doing, or what their plans were.

He and Christopher had talked about leaving to join a ship. The plan was to get hired to a merchant ship. They asked different merchant captains if they were hiring, but none had been willing to yet. Christopher had been offered one job, but he didn't take it because there wasn't a job for Henry.

"Surely someone would hire them soon," Henry mulled as they walked up the steps to the house and went inside.

"Henry, please bring in some more firewood," his mother said from the kitchen when she heard them enter. "Joanna, where have you been? I told you to finish scrubbing the kitchen floor."

"Yes, mother."

Henry went out to the wood pile, bringing a large armload back with him. to gather an armload before taking it back into the kitchen.

"Thank you, son," she smiled at him. He studied his mother for a moment as he thought of her hurt when he finally disappeared. The guilt stuck in his throat like dry bread and he quickly turned to walk out of the kitchen but stopped when Joanna got in his way.

"Feeling guilty?" she whispered.

"I'm fine, actually," he lied to her with a smile.

"I don't believe you," she said, raising her eyebrows knowingly. "You know what she'll say when you take off in the night."

"You're just jealous you can't come along. You have to stay here and be the dutiful daughter who marries someone Father approves of. Instead of Chris," he smirked at her, his eyes flashing with amusement.

Joanna looked at him with surprise.

"I loath Chris! Why would you say such a ridiculous thing?!" she protested indignantly. He knew her better though.

"I've seen the way you look at him. If you're not snubbing him, you're staring at him. Like all the other shallow girls," he shook his head as her face turned to anger.

"How dare you!" she spat.

"It's true, I'll be sad to leave Mother. But don't worry. I've already written a letter telling her everything, and of Chris's love for her too."

"What, no letter for Father?" sarcasm nearly dripped from her rosy lips as she smirked at him.

"I have one for him too. Explaining my desire to go to sea instead of becoming a minister of the church."

"He'll hate it."

Henry shrugged, "I don't care. I won't be here to listen to what he says about it." Then he leaned closer and his eyes became dreamy as he thought of the future. "I'll be meeting new and interesting people, in new and interesting places. I won't have a care in the world." As long as he wasn't caught as a pirate, but she didn't know that part. She just knew they wanted to become sailors after learning of their plans when she found them practicing swords at the river.

Joanna grew serious for a moment.

"I'm going to miss you too. I wish you'd stay," she said softly. Then a faraway dreamy look came to her eyes, "Or that I could go as well."

Henry looked at her with surprise. She had never said anything like that.

She walked into the kitchen before he could reply, and he watched her curiously for a moment before turning and walking towards his room thoughtfully.

Christopher wiped the table off before taking the plates to the kitchen. Christopher had done so well working off Saul's debt that Mr. Brown had kept him on at the tavern. He knew all of the regulars who came in, and he was liked by all. The sailors who came in told him stories that made him long for the day a captain took him on as a hand.

Thankfully his father didn't seem to care about his job at the tavern. Nothing changed with his father. They still hated each other and Christopher only stayed at the house when it was too cold to sleep at the river, which is what he had to do this night since it was so cold that the river had ice floating along in it. He dreaded going home to his father though.

"Boy. More ale here," A man shouted across the room.

"And bring a mug for my captain."

Christopher picked up a pitcher of ale and a mug before moving to the table where he served them. As he poured the mug of ale for the new man at the table, he looked at him.

"You're a captain, sir?"

"Yes," the man looked at Christopher and took off his hat to reveal long blond hair tied back.

"I don't suppose you'd be taking on any new men while you're here?" Christopher asked confidently.

"Maybe. I lost a few men in my last run to Europe." The captain looked at him seriously. "You offering?"

Christopher nodded, "Yes, sir. My friend and I are looking to join up on a ship."

The captain looked at his ale and took a drink before looking back at Christopher.

"I could use a couple of swabbies, but it's hard work, and I expect a lot of out of you."

Christopher smiled, "Yes, sir. We'll be glad to work."

"Fine. Be at the docks on Tuesday morning. The ship Maria."

"Yes, sir," Christopher grinned.

The captain looked over at one of the men at the table and started talking to the man. Feeling dismissed, Christopher turned and went towards the kitchen. He couldn't wait to tell Henry! Their dream was finally coming true!

"Henry, I've found us a captain!" Christopher exclaimed as he walked up to Henry who was outside chopping wood.

"You have?!" Henry asked with wide eyes.

Christopher grinned as he clapped Henry's shoulder.

"It's happening, Henry!"

"When?" Henry asked with a grin in return.

"Tomorrow. We're to be at the docks in the morning."

Henry nodded, "I'll be ready."

"Let's spend our last day by the river instead of at the docks," Christopher said.

Henry nodded, and they left without seeing Joanna move behind the curtain at the window above them.

They spent the day at the river sparring, sitting by the river eating their dinner, and talking about how their plans were starting to become reality.

But as Henry ate supper with his family, he realized what he was about to leave behind the next morning, and he felt a tightening in his chest. It was going to be harder to leave his family than he had dreamed it to be. He always thought it would be freeing to leave and not look back. But the next morning when he was up before dawn packing a small knot formed in his stomach. He left the letters for his parents on his bed. When he finished he put his bag outside the front door before taking some wood to the kitchen for his mother, and she was already there making breakfast.

"Good morning, dear. You're up a little early," she said.

"Yes, I promised Chris I'd meet him."

The partial lie tasted bitter. Henry watched her move to the fireplace where she took out four hot biscuits and placed them on a towel.

"Well, take these with you, dear. I can't have my boys going hungry," she handed him the towel with a loving smile, and he smiled a little in return.

Then without thinking, he hugged her.

"Thank you, mother. I love you."

She hugged him in return.

"Well, I love you too, son. Have a good day."

Henry released her and turned away quickly so she wouldn't see the emotion that threatened to give him away.

"Goodbye, Mother." He looked at her a little longer than usual to memorize her face, knowing he might never see her again.

Then he went through the door and picked up his bag before walking towards the river.

Christopher didn't have much to pack, only a few shirts

and pants. He grabbed all he had and put it in his old bag. He was stuffing a shirt in when he heard the noises of his father getting up. The drunk man stumbled into the kitchen holding a bottle.

"What are you doing to make so much noise, boy?" his father growled.

Christopher stepped back as he tied the bag closed.

"Sorry, Pa."

Suddenly his father reached out and grabbed the bag from Christopher.

"What's this for?" he asked before taking another drink from the almost empty bottle.

"Nothing, Pa," Christopher tried to reach out and take it back but his father turned and the bag moved further away. "Pa, I need that."

"You go'n somewhere, boy?"

"Yes, Pa, and I'm never coming back," Christopher jutted out his chin in defiance and held out his hand to indicate he wanted his bag back.

"You ungrateful brat. I oughta whip you for thinking anything here belongs to you. I gave you all of this. It's mine." His father stepped closer, menacingly, and Christopher tried not to back down despite flinching at his father's every move.

"I acquired those myself, Pa, they're mine," Christopher felt anger rise in his chest. "Give me the bag, Pa," he said firmly.

His father snickered, "Tough guy, eh? You won't last five minutes out there without me. You ungrateful boy. I oughta teach you a lesson," his father swung the bottle at Christopher.

Christopher ducked and his anger flared. He had dealt with his father for years, and was tired of letting the evil man get the best of him! Christopher reached out as he stood back up and grabbed the bottle. It didn't take much effort to take the bottle from his father's hand. Then Christopher smashed the bottle to bits over his father's head! The man crumpled to the ground instantly. Blood trickled down his father's head and onto his face.

The man was still as a stone, and Christopher couldn't see

him breathing. Fear rose in him and he grabbed his bag before fleeing the house!

"Did I just kill my own father?!" he ran faster until he reached the river where he found the spot empty. Henry hadn't made it yet.

Christopher took a minute to let the shock settle. He had just killed his greatest fear! Part of him was scared someone would come after him and arrest him. But as his breathing slowed and he thought more clearly, he realized he was free of the man he hated for so long!

"He can't hurt me or anyone else anymore!" He dwelled on the thought until he started to realize a new sense of freedom that brought him relief. He stood a little taller. *"No more getting beaten! I'm free to start a new life with no fear!"*

He went to the hiding spot where he kept his extra shirt and pants, and then picked up the swords. He was finally feeling calmer as Henry walked up. Henry didn't look excited or happy, just thoughtful with a frown.

"Having second thoughts?" Christopher asked him with narrowed eyes.

Henry looked at him with surprise, "No, of course not."

Christopher nodded, "Good. Let's get to the docks."

The young men hurried towards the wharf until they found the Dutch fluet, Maria, and walked up the gangplank. Sailors were everywhere getting ready to sail the large ship.

"You must be our new swabbies."

They turned to find a man of about thirty, with a full brown beard, brown hair, and dark blue eyes who looked them over with judgment.

"Yes, sir," Christopher answered.

"I'm Quartermaster Tolls. I expect your best without question. Understand?"

"Yes, sir," Christopher stood tall and nodded confidently.

Henry followed Christopher's example and nodded, "Yes, sir."

"That man over there with the black shirt and blue vest is

the boatswain, Robert. Introduce yourselves. He'll give you most of your orders."

The boys looked where the quartermaster pointed to a man working at the side of the ship. As the quartermaster walked away, the boys walked to the boatswain.

"Sir? We've been told to report to you," Christopher said.

Robert looked at the two young men in front of him, and shook his head, *"They look too neat to be sailors,"* he thought. Then asked them with a frown, "Who are you?"

"We've just been hired on," the tallest one with black hair said and his friend nodded. "We're eager to get started, sir."

Robert looked them over carefully.

"What are your names."

The tall dark-haired boy straightened seriously.

"I'm Christopher. This is Henry. The captain hired us himself."

Robert still looked at them seriously. The slightly shorter young man with light brown hair and green eyes that reminded him of his own boy whom he hadn't seen in years, looked like he belonged in a more reputable profession. Robert sighed slightly.

"The captain's right. We need swabbies, but it's hard work."

"We'll work hard, sir," Henry said with a slight smile.

"You'll have to," Robert looked from the bags to the swords in their hands, "Do you know how to use those?"

"Yes, sir. We've been training with them for about five years now." Christopher said.

Robert looked at them with narrow eyes.

"Have you ever killed anyone with them?"

They became serious, and Henry shook his head no. But it was Christopher's reaction that caught Robert's attention. He suddenly looked nervous and didn't deny anything. Robert raised an eyebrow slightly.

"Alright. Follow me. I'll show you where to stow your gear."

Robert waved for them to follow and Henry smiled as he followed Christopher and Robert down below the decks.

"You'll have to make yourselves a place to sleep on the floor. We don't have enough hammocks for you right now."

Henry was glad he had brought a blanket with him. They dropped their bags and swords on the floor where they would sleep.

"I don't have time to teach you anything right now. Just stay out of the way of the crew as we set sail. Once we're underway, I'll show you your first task."

"Yes, sir," Henry said with a nod as Robert walked away. Then he turned to Christopher. "Let's go up on deck and watch them get underway."

Christopher nodded and they found a railing at the end of the ship where they could watch without being in the way of the sailors.

Suddenly, Henry heard his name being called and he turned to look at the docks. Joanna was on the street yelling at him with a frown.

"Henry!"

"Joanna? What are you doing here?" he yelled to her.

"You can't leave, Henry. Please, stay!"

"I can't," he felt a little compassion as he watched her tears fall, "I'm sorry I didn't come to find you before I boarded. Don't worry, though. We're going to be great."

"Will you come back?" she asked.

"I don't know," his voice became stronger as he yelled back an order, "Go home. Be happy, Joanna."

She shook her head with sorrow and then looked at Christopher standing next to Henry.

"Chris, take care of Henry," she demanded.

Christopher smiled slightly and nodded, "Goodbye, Joanna."

She stood watching them as she wiped at the falling tears futilely.

"Go, Joanna," Henry said firmly and pointed towards

home.

She nodded slightly as she started walking home. She looked back once more before she turned the corner at the end of the street and disappeared.

Christopher looked at Henry seriously.

"It's not too late to stay," he said to Henry.

Henry shook his head, "I don't want to stay. You?"

Christopher shook his head and the boys watched together as the ship set sail. They watched the shoreline of Carolsport fade away until there was nothing left to look at. They had done it. They were on their first voyage.

Chapter 3

"Alright, men," Robert came up beside them. "Come with me."

Christopher and Henry followed him to a couple of buckets and mops sitting in the corner.

"You're swabbies now. If you're not doing something for the crew, then you're swabbing the decks. Seaweed gets on the ship and mold will grow if we let it. They need to be cleaned off. Get used to it, because you'll be doing it a lot," Robert said as he handed each of them a mop. "When you run out of seawater, get more and do it again. Get to work."

Henry and Christopher looked at each other, and after a minute, they grinned as they dipped their mops into the water buckets.

At first, Christopher didn't mind the work. It didn't seem all that hard. Then his hands started to become sore. By the time they stopped that evening for supper, his hands were hurting from working with the rough mop handle.

"Ouch," Henry said softly as he lowered himself down onto his blanket after supper. He looked at his blistered hands with a wince.

Christopher took his blanket out and spread it down next to Henry's.

"Don't show you're hurt," he said to Henry as he glanced around.

"No one is here. It's just us," Henry laid down with a shrug.

"Doesn't matter. We've got to learn not to show weakness," Christopher lowered his voice, "These sailors are tough, but pirates will be worse," he shook his head, "No fear, no weakness, Henry."

Henry looked at his friend seriously and nodded once. Then he turned onto his side away from Christopher. Guilt at leaving his family came as the tiredness settled in, and he shoved the emotion back down his throat. He had made his choice, and it was a good one. He knew it was. He had dreamed of it for years, and now his dreams were coming true. The only thing he'd be from now on was happy. Happy no matter what he had to do. There was no going back now.

Christopher stared at the ceiling and listened to the men who came in talking. They were drinking and one man was telling a story about some pirates he'd met. Christopher listened for a short time but soon closed his eyes as tiredness set in. Then his father came to his mind. He hated the man, but he wasn't sure how he felt about killing his own father. He knew he should feel guilty, but all he felt was relief. He was rid of the evil man. He had nothing left to go back to Carolsport for now. No reason to look back.

∞∞∞

"Well, men, I think you've proven to be hard workers. You've been swabbing decks from morning to night, for at least a month. We'll be pulling into the port of Brighton, England soon. You'll be helping unload the cargo we have in the hold, then help load the new cargo. After that, all men will have shore leave for a couple of days. When you're back on board you'll be taking on more responsibilities. You'll be helping the cook, taking meals to the officers, and standing watch. Understand?" Robert asked sternly.

"Yes, sir," Christopher said seriously.

"Yes, sir," Henry smiled.

"We should be in Brighton tomorrow."

Robert walked away and Christopher looked at Henry's smiling face.

"What?"

"We made it to our first port," Henry said as his smile turned to a grin.

"Well, don't give us bad luck by saying so before we actually dock," Christopher shook his head at his friend.

The hard work was starting to fill them out and their muscles were strengthening. Christopher felt good with the work and his new life at sea. Henry had expressed the same thoughts over the last month.

They hadn't run into any pirates along the journey to England, but they had agreed they should learn all they could before they joined a pirate ship.

The next day dawned with land being called out from the crow's nest. As soon as they docked, the men went to work unloading cargo.

Robert watched the two young men working. Christopher and Henry worked as hard as any other man in the crew. He could see them being quite useful and he was impressed with them.

When the cargo was unloaded, the young men didn't even seem tired. Robert nodded as he decided something. He walked over to them and caught their attention.

"The captain said the cargo won't be ready for loading for another couple of days. We've been granted shore leave tonight and tomorrow." Robert explained sternly. "You'll get your pay tonight. If you want a place to spend it, most of us will be headed to a tavern not far from here. They have good food and ale. Worth spending your first pay."

Christopher nodded, "Thank you, sir. We'd like to come."

Henry grinned, "Yes, sir."

That evening as the sun was setting the captain paid each man.

Henry grinned, "We made it, Chris."

Christopher nodded, "Yes, and it's worth it every hard day." He reached over and punched Henry lightly on the shoulder. "Let's keep up with the men tonight."

"What do you mean?" Henry looked at him like he'd said something funny, "If you mean walking to the tavern I'm sure we'll have no problem."

Christopher shook his head a little.

"No, I mean if we're going to be sailors then we should celebrate and live like the other sailors."

Henry nodded and grinned, "Bet I can drink more ale than you."

Christopher grew serious, "If I'm like my father, then you probably can."

Henry's smile disappeared.

"You're not your father, Chris. You're nothing like him." Henry put his hand on his friend's shoulder and squeezed it hard to make his point. Then he punched Christopher's arm, and his smile returned. "Come on. Let's go. They're leaving."

They followed about half the crew and Robert towards a tavern only a few blocks from the docks. They stepped into a warm big room filled with tables and chairs. A roaring fire blazed in the big fireplace. There were a few patrons, but the crew filled a good portion of the room when they entered.

Christopher and Henry sat down at a table with Robert and Cale.

Movement from the counter drew his gaze to a beautiful woman with curly dark brown hair and blue eyes. He felt something akin to hunger stir inside him. As she came over carrying mugs and a pitcher, he watched her move with purpose.

"Ale, boys?" she asked in a stern tone.

"Ah, Miss Sophie, you know we do," Cale said from Robert's side with a grin. "We brought some new boys to meet you, Miss Sophie. This is Henry and Christopher."

She looked over Christopher and Henry with a slight smile as her gaze lingered on Christopher. He looked at her in return, but she couldn't read his face.

"You boys are new to this life aren't you?" she said perceptively.

"Yes, ma'am," Henry said smiling.

"Don't ruin them," she said to Robert and Cale seriously.

"We wouldn't do that," Cale said with a smirk.

She shook her head as she poured mugs of ale for the four of them.

"We'd like whatever you're cook'n tonight too, Miss Sophie," Robert said seriously.

"Just don't cause me any problems. Remember the rules. Fighting gets you kicked out." She gave Cale a pointed look that said she was talking to him specifically.

Cale feigned a wounded heart. "I'd never cause you problems, Miss Sophie."

Sophie looked at him knowingly.

"How do you like my new table? I had to get it after your last visit, Cale," She patted the table with her free hand.

"It's a beauty," Cale said with a grin, "I'm honored to eat at it."

Sophie put her hand on the table and leaned towards Cale with a stern look.

"Break my table again and you're buying me two," she said.

"Yes, ma'am." Cale winked at her.

She stood back up and put her hand on her hip, then she looked at Christopher and Henry again.

"And don't take after him. He's a bad influence."

The young men nodded with amusement, and she turned and walked away.

Christopher looked at the mug of ale in front of him. Part of him wanted to stay away from the stuff. He didn't want to end up like his father. But he knew if he was to be part of the crew it was something he needed to do. He picked up the mug and sighed internally.

"Here goes," he thought before he took a big swallow of the

ale. A warmth came over him as the ale settled in his stomach. The taste was tolerable. He took another drink before realizing Henry was staring at him. Christopher shrugged his indifference and Henry took a drink of his own mug.

Sophie came back with bowls of stew for them all and they ate hungrily. Henry suddenly felt a pang of homesickness eating the food. His mother's cooking was something he missed often. It was the best thing they had tasted since leaving home. Rations were filling but bland. He took another drink to swallow the emotions of homesickness and guilt he got as he thought of his mother. The emotions had lessened some over the last month, but the food was bringing it all back. The memory of his loving mother made him smile a little at memories of her.

"What are you smiling about now?" Cale shook his head at Henry. "He's always smiling. What do you have to be so happy about?"

Henry was taken off guard and didn't answer quickly enough.

"I was just thinking this stew reminds me of his mother's stew," Christopher spoke up. "She made the best stew. I might have to have more. Makes rations taste like dirt."

Part of Henry was irritated Christopher brought up his mother in front of the sailors. It didn't seem right. He gave Christopher a little glare when he met his gaze. Christopher looked at him with confusion.

"Homesick are you boys?" Cale grinned.

"No," Henry said firmly before taking another bite.

Cale let out a boisterous laugh and slapped the table, making the plates and mugs jump a little.

"Don't worry about it boys. It'll ease the longer you're away," Robert said kindly before taking a drink.

"Maybe we should drop them off at home on our next crossing," Cale said with amusement.

"Give it a rest, Cale," Robert said, "They're young. They'll learn."

The door opened and three rough-looking sailors walked

in. They looked around and glared at the almost full room. Then they sat down at a table and one pounded his fist on the table.

"Sophie!" he shouted, "Get out here! We want food and ale!"

Sophie came from the kitchen and looked at them with scorn.

"I thought I told you to stay out of here you scum. You're not welcome here."

"Who's going to make me leave? Get us some food and ale," The man demanded menacingly.

Sophie shook her head but brought the three men ale.

Cale shook his head.

"She shouldn't have to put up with that pirate," he said with a growl.

"Don't start anything. Sophie will kick you out," Robert said, taking another bite of stew.

Henry and Christopher watched with curiosity.

"They are pirates?" Christopher asked.

"Could be," Robert said, "There's a ship in the dock that is suspected of piracy. There's no real evidence though. I've just heard tales."

"What ship?" asked Henry calmly.

Robert looked at them knowingly.

"I won't say. Can't have you leaving to join up with them. Pirates hang, boys. You don't want to be associated with that lot."

"Who said we wanted to be pirates?" Henry said with a shrug, "Just curious."

Robert looked at him knowingly again, "Sure."

They watched as Sophie brought the three men their food. The man who had demanded food grinned at Sophie and put an arm around her waist, pulling her towards him.

"Let me go!" she said firmly. When he didn't, she squirmed as he pulled her down on his lap. "Let me go!"

Christopher could hear the fear in her voice and he grimaced.

Cale suddenly started to move, but Robert pulled him back.

"She said no roughing. You'll get us kicked out."

Cale looked annoyed.

"Maybe Cale would, but I doubt she'd kick us out," Christopher surprised them as he spoke up. He nodded to Henry and Henry nodded back.

They stood up and walked together over to the table and glared at the man holding Sophie and laughing. Sophie shook her head when she saw them.

"I can take care of myself," she said sternly.

"I can see that," Christopher said wryly to her. Then he tapped the man's shoulder to get his attention, "The lady asked you to let her go."

The man glared at them with an evil smile.

"Who's going to make me? A couple of boys?" the man laughed and tightened his grip on Sophie so she flinched.

"You wouldn't find it as easy as you think to deal with us," Christopher said firmly.

The man laughed again, but before he could stop Henry punched the man in the face as hard as he could. The man slumped onto the table unconscious. Christopher grabbed Sophie's wrist, pulled her up, and flung her behind him. Christopher braced himself as the two other men came around the table menacingly.

No one spoke, they just glared at each other for a moment. Christopher glanced at Henry for a second and realized his mistake as a fist landed on his jaw. Christopher staggered back a step before regaining his balance, then delivered a torrent of punches back with fervor. Henry didn't wait, launching an attack on the man in front of him as soon as he saw the attack on Christopher. Henry's opponent went still and Henry stepped back. The sight of his companion down caused Christopher's opponent to become distracted. Christopher grabbed the man's arm and wrenched his arm behind his back before pushing him down on the table.

"Get out, and don't come back," Christopher growled. He released him and stepped back. The man nearly ran from the tavern. Christopher looked at Henry, "Let's get them out of here."

They dragged the men out and dropped them in the middle of the street. They went back in to find the whole tavern talking excitedly. Their crew broke out with smiles and laughter. Some got up and congratulated Christopher and Henry on a good fight, especially Henry, whose fury of punches had impressed them. Christopher saw Sophie glaring at them and he walked over to her.

"I told you I can take care of myself," she said irritably.

"I never said you couldn't. We just wanted to help," he smiled at her bravado. "I suppose you want us to leave, even though we didn't break a table."

She stared at him a moment before replying.

"I told you no fighting. But you haven't finished your supper. You can stay to do that and then you go."

"Thank you. We'd like that. Your food is the best we've had in a month." he said softly as he looked into her blue eyes. A brown curl of hair fell into her face and he reached out to tuck a piece behind her ear.

She looked at him with surprise at his gentleness, and she blushed a little.

"I'll get you more stew," she said softly before turning to walk away quickly.

He watched her go and then turned to sit down at the table with Henry, Robert, and Cale.

"We didn't know you boys could fight like that," Cale said with a grin.

"You mean men. I think they just proved themselves to be men," Robert said with a nod to them.

Cale nodded and raised his mug.

"To the fine young men we have to sail with. No pirate will defeat them."

The other crewmen raised their mugs in agreement.

Christopher nodded his appreciation and looked over to

see Henry grinning like a fool.

The men went back to eating as Sophie walked up and set bowls of fresh stew in front of him and Henry. He looked up at her.

"Thank you," he said with a nod.

She looked at him funny and he wondered what she was thinking. When she caught his eye, she quickly finished placing bowls around the table.

"I'll bring you more ale," and she left swiftly.

The men talked over stew and ale late into the night. Christopher acted like Sophie didn't affect him every time she came to give them more ale or food, but he couldn't help admiring her more and more as the evening wore on. Finally, the men decided they should get back to the ship and started to leave. They laid their money on the table and after he had done so, Christopher walked over to Sophie, who was cleaning a table. She stopped as he walked up behind her.

"I just wanted to say thank you for the good food. If I'm not banned from your tavern I'd like to come back," he said softly.

Sophie turned to find Christopher standing close and she looked up at him, trying to be serious.

"As long as you don't break a table," she said softly.

He nodded but didn't move away.

Sophie couldn't breathe let alone move away from his handsome figure. She stared up into his piercing blue eyes and felt herself gently melt. He reached out, took her chin in his hand, and leaned down to kiss her softly. Then he moved back a step and turned to follow the others out the door.

She stood for a moment in stunned silence. Her fingers moved to her lips as she remembered his soft kiss. No one had ever treated her with such kindness and care before. She suddenly couldn't wait to see him the next day, and she smiled.

Chapter 4

Christopher couldn't figure out how he felt about Sophie. She was beautiful. Maybe even more beautiful than Joanna. Sophie's lips were soft and tasted of her fine bread she served with her stew. She must be hard working and quite intelligent to have her own tavern at a young age and run it on her own. He admired her for that.

But the ship would be leaving soon. And so would he.

As he watched her serve others around the room, he wanted nothing more than to kiss her again. If she rejected his advances he decided that was fine with him. There would be other Sophies in other towns, but he would still try to win her affection.

That evening he stayed until everyone, including Henry, had left. She came to him with a stern look.

"I'm ready to close up for the night," she said. "Aren't you leaving? Your friend already did."

He stared at her intently and she stepped closer to pick up his mug.

"Do you want more ale?" she asked without looking at him.

Christopher reached out and took the mug out of her hand, and set it back on the table. He took the pitcher from her other hand and set it on the table as well. Taking her hands in his, Christopher pulled Sophie to himself until she was sitting on his lap. He released her hands and moved one around her waist. The other hand moved up behind her neck, and he pulled her down for a kiss. The kiss intensified and he moved his other hand to her neck, holding her tightly. Her hands clenched his shirt as she kissed him back.

She stopped, trying to catch her breath, but he pulled her back for more. She moved her face to the side and he kissed her neck. She felt herself grow warm and breathless, and she moved to kiss him again.

Christopher absent-mindedly moved his lips down her neck almost of their own accord. At the same time, his fingers found the ribbon that tied her bodice and pulled it. It loosened and he pulled the other. His lips moved down to the top of her loose bodice, but suddenly she stood and stepped away before he could catch her. He looked at her, stupefied.

She shook her head. "No. You have to leave," she said firmly as she walked towards another table, shakily gathering the dishes.

He quickly rose and went to her. Putting his hands around her waist.

"Why?" he asked softly before he kissed her neck again.

"You're leaving and I'll probably never see you again. I can't ask you to stay in Brighton, and I know you won't even if I do, so you should go now."

He heard the dishes clink as she put them back down on the table. He reached around her head and pulled her to turn towards him. He leaned down to kiss her again and again until she pulled away. This time he saw tears coming down her cheeks.

"Please, leave," she said softly.

He frowned as his thumb rubbed the spot behind her ear.

"What if I want to stay?" he said softly.

She shook her head firmly.

"I want you to leave. Now. And don't come back," she said as she choked on her tears.

"Please, Sophie, let me stay," he leaned down to kiss her again, but she pulled herself out of his grasp and backed away.

"Get out," she demanded.

"Sophie, I can't," he moved to her but before he could take her in his arms again she slapped him hard across the face.

"Get out, Christopher," she backed away until there was a table between them.

Anger rose inside Christopher.

"Fine," he stalked out the door without looking back.

He started walking back toward the docks. The anger at her rejection stung. If he ever returned to Brighton, he would be sure his shadow not fall on her doorstep. He would gladly eat rations for a month before sitting at her table again.

Suddenly, a hand clapped on his shoulder and spun him around. The next thing he knew a fist smashed into his face, and he fell to the ground. Fists and boots pounded on him. He tried to rise, but he grew weaker with each blow. Soon he blacked out completely.

When he woke, Christopher found himself lying in the muddy street in the pouring rain. He slowly sat up identifying every bruise on his body as he moved. It all ached with pain, and his ribs hurt the most. He slowly got to his feet and shook his head a little. He wiped at the water on his face. Then he slowly made his way towards the docks.

He came up on the ship as the crew was loading cargo.

"Where have you been?" Robert asked with a frown when he saw Christopher.

"Nowhere," Christopher said gruffly, holding onto a spot on his ribs.

"You should have stuck with the crew instead of staying late at the tavern. Hope she was worth the beating," Robert said wryly.

Christopher didn't answer. How did Robert know? He must be more bruised than he realized. He wasn't sure if it'd been worth it or not. He didn't want to think about it.

"Where do you want me?" he asked Robert.

"Help load the cargo. If you can." Robert shook his head and walked away.

Christopher grimaced with each step as he walked towards the men to help. It was difficult and slow going since his ribs hurt the most. By the time they were done, he was aching. He went down to eat his rations and then collapsed on his blanket.

"You don't look so good," Henry said as he walked up and looked down at him. "You're covered in mud."

"Yes, I know. I'll clean up after I rest."

"What happened to you last night? You never made it back."

"Someone gave me a beating on my way back. I didn't wake until this morning."

Henry nodded, "Well you look like a sight. Maybe you should freshen up a bit before you go meet her."

"What?" Christopher looked at him with confusion.

"Sophie. She's waiting for you on the dock."

Christopher sat up quickly with a grimace.

"Why didn't you say something sooner you oaf?" he said gruffly as he rose and slicked back his black hair with one hand as he started for the stairs.

He made his way onto the main deck and walked towards the dock, where Sophie stood with the hood of her cloak over her head to keep the rain off. He walked down the plank and stopped in front of her. He didn't say anything, just stood there in the rain staring at her with irritation. Why bother seeking him out when he was shipbound?

"I just wanted to see you before you left," she said softly.

"Well, you've seen me. Is that all?" he said sternly.

She looked at the ground, hurt. When she looked back up at him, he saw the tears running down her face, and his heart softened slightly.

"I just wanted to say I'm sorry," she said frowning crossly.

Christopher stepped to her and took her face in his hands before kissing her deeply. When he stopped he rested his head against hers gently.

"Can you come to the tavern tonight?" she asked.

"No, we sail in the morning and we're not allowed to leave."

He kissed her again before standing back up straight.

"I'm sorry I chased you away last night," she said as tears rolled down her cheeks and mixed with the rain on her face.

Christopher nodded slightly as he rubbed his thumb along her mouth.

Sophie sniffed as she stared at him, longing to beg him to stay, but knowing he wouldn't. She shivered as the rain soaked through her cloak.

"You should go home before you get sick," he said gently.

"I wish I could stay here with you forever," she said as she threw herself into his arms. He moved his arms around her and she put her head on his chest. "Please come back."

Christopher didn't respond. He had no intention to come back for her. He held her for a moment before firmly kissing her once more before he stepped away and let her go.

He walked back up the plank and out of sight feeling her eyes on him as he walked away.

Sophie didn't know if she was shaking from cold or sorrow. Her heart kept her from crying out to him, pleading with him to come back to her. His mind was filled with ocean dreams and his blood was cut with salt water. He would never stay on land for her, and her heart knew this.

Christopher changed his clothes before lying down and staring at the ceiling above.

"What did she want?" Henry asked.

Christopher looked at him, "To say goodbye."

Henry grinned.

"What?" Christopher asked with a frown.

"Only here a couple of days and you made a girl fall in love with you."

Christopher shook his head a little, "Sophie is no girl."

"So I noticed," Henry said wryly, "She's old enough to own her own tavern. She's no young miss for sure. Yet, she was taken in by your charms. Just like all the others who fall at your feet."

Christopher didn't reply.

"Would you have stayed if she'd asked you? Do you love her?" Henry's question was odd. He should know Christopher wouldn't stay. Nor did he love Sophie. Her warm arms and soft lips were what pulled him to her.

Christopher shook his head with annoyance. "I don't know anything about love. And no, I wouldn't stay."

Henry nodded thoughtfully, "Good."

Christopher looked at Henry wryly before closing his eyes to rest and fell asleep to the image of Sophie's lips moving up to meet his.

∞∞∞

"I've been trying to teach them how to watch for storms but we haven't had anything but a little rain since they came on board. I wouldn't rely on them to tell you when a storm is coming, sir," Robert explained to Captain Skork.

"Alright," the captain ran his hand through his blond hair and replaced the hat on his head. "Have someone sit with them on their shifts to show them what to look for. How else are they working out? I noticed you gave them more responsibilities."

"Yes, sir, they work hard with no complaint, and I think they are doing just fine."

"Good, I was concerned they might be too green when I hired them on."

"They have proven they have some value, already. That fight they got into in Brighton was won without breaking a sweat. The three men were older, more experienced, and rather rough. But those two boys fought together with precision. They came with swords, too. If they know how to use them as well as they can use their fists, then I'd say they are valuable assets."

The captain nodded thoughtfully. "This is a good report. You may go, thank you."

"Yes, sir."

Robert looked up at the crow's nest as he left the captain's cabin. Henry was sitting with a ridiculous grin like always. Robert shook his head in amusement and continued on his mission to find Brack. Robert smirked at the thought of all the new words he would learn when Brack learned of his new work detail.

He walked down to the lower deck and found Brack eating his rations.

"Brack, I need you to sit with Henry in the crow's nest and teach him how to watch for storms. Your shift will be his now."

"Why me?" Brack grumbled.

"Because you're the best at recognizing a storm coming before anyone else." Then Robert looked at Cale, "You're to do the same with Christopher."

Christopher looked up at him when he heard his name and frowned.

"Alright," Cale said with a nod, "Are you expecting there to be a storm?"

"It's been too long since we ran into one, and it's the season for them."

Cale nodded.

Robert walked back out of the room and Christopher looked down at the pot of rations he'd been serving from.

Surely watching for a storm wasn't that big of a deal. You can see black clouds from a long way off. Plenty of time to be ready for it. At least he liked Cale and found he wasn't such a bad guy to be around. He spooned some rations into a bowl for another sailor.

∞∞∞

Brack pulled himself into the nest with a grunt and shoved Henry to make him move over.

"Is my shift over already?" Henry asked as he moved over to make room for Brack.

"No," Brack growled, "I've been commanded to teach you how to watch for storms."

"Ah, good," Henry nodded with a grin. "I've just been sitting here watching the horizon thinking. I didn't know there were things to watch for other than black clouds."

Brack grunted, "You're a fool."

Henry grinned, "I have a lot to learn."

Brack just looked around them as he watched the horizon.

"Your mate Christopher sure had that pretty lady from the tavern bedeviled."

Henry nodded, "Yeah, he didn't tell me much about her, but he seemed to be preoccupied with her. All that matters is that Christopher didn't care enough about her to stay in England. If he was engrossed with Sophie, yet still wouldn't stay with her, then I doubt any woman would get him to stay on land."

Brack smirked, "What of yourself? Would you let a female keep you on land?"

"No," Henry laughed, "I love sea life. I wanted nothing more than to spend my life on the blue waters." He watched the sun setting in the far distance as it mixed with the dark blue of the waters. It was a mesmerizing sight.

Henry looked around in a circle to check for any ships that may be near them, but he didn't see anything. Christopher was jealous it wasn't his shift for watch and was stuck helping the cook down below. Christopher's least favorite task and it wasn't something Henry liked either. Sitting in the crow's nest was easily becoming his favorite job. It was amazing to be so high up above the water like the birds. He grinned as he went back to watching the sunset and thinking about flying over the ocean like a bird. If anything would be better than sailing, it'd be flying.

Chapter 5

"So you fell for Sophie's stew did you?" Cale said with a grin as they sat in the crow's nest the next evening.

Christopher didn't acknowledge Cale's question. He just looked out at the horizon.

"I saw you kiss her before we left the tavern that night, and again on the dock. I was mostly surprised she let you. She doesn't usually let her guard down with sailors, seeing as we are all a sinful lot."

Still, Christopher didn't respond to Cale's comment.

"Well?"

Christopher looked at Cale and frowned, "Why would I tell you anything?"

"Just curious. Every sailor that docks in Brighton wants to kiss that woman," Cale looked at Christopher closely. "You succeeded where many others have failed. What do you have to offer that other men don't?"

Christopher looked back out over the horizon and shrugged.

"Nothing. She was pretty so I kissed her," he said simply.

Cale looked at him in surprise, "That's it?"

"If I loved her I wouldn't have left. Would I?"

Cale shook his head, "You can leave someone you love, I have."

Now Christopher looked surprised.

Cale looked out over the horizon thoughtfully.

"Her name was Lily. Curly golden hair and soft green eyes. She was the very picture of a lady. The ship I had been working on was docked for repairs after a storm. I met her and we spent every moment of those two weeks together. When it came time to leave she asked me to stay. I thought about it all for one minute and told her I couldn't. She cried. I left. I've never seen her since. I think of her often enough and it keeps me warm on cold nights. And if you promise not to tell anyone I'll tell you something else."

Cale looked at him sternly and Christopher raised his brow in question.

"Every time we're in port, I send her a letter. I tell her about my life at sea and tell her I miss her, but I always end it by telling her not to wait for me. That I'll never make it back to her. I've not been back in the three years since."

Christopher thought about what Cale had said.

"I don't think Sophie and I had anything worth writing letters over. It'd be easier to forget it."

Cale looked at the young man thoughtfully and then nodded. He'd let it go, though he wasn't sure what to think. Sophie had always been good to him, and he hated seeing her taken in by this young man who didn't seem to care about her much. He had seen them on the dock before sailing and he couldn't help the slight irritation he felt towards Christopher's indifference. But he'd have to put his concerns aside. It wasn't his business.

They sat quietly watching the sky as the sun but a shiny sliver.

"There," Cale pointed to the north and they could barely make out a cloud that suddenly had a small flash of light ripple through it.

"A storm," Christopher frowned. "Will it be big?"

"No telling yet. We'll just have to watch it."

Cale leaned over the edge of the crow's nest and whistled to Quartermaster Tolls. Cale pointed towards the storm and everyone turned to look.

When the quartermaster saw the lightning ripple through the sky, he hurried to the captain's cabin. The captain came out and they walked up to the top deck.

"Any idea what direction it's headed?" Captain Skork asked Tolls as they watched the lightning.

"Not sure, might be moving southeast. It's just hard to tell since it's still growing, and now it's dark."

Captain nodded, "Alright, let's go straight west as fast as possible. If we can get clear of it then we'd be better off."

"We're still south of it, and it's headed right for us. Do you think we can get out of the way in time, sir?"

"We have to try, Tolls."

"Yes, sir," Tolls turned to look out over the ship, "Let all the sails out," he yelled as he walked to take the place at the helm. He turned the ship to go straight towards the west.

Men came alive as they scurried up the mast to let out all the sails and tie things off.

As Henry tied a knot in a rope, he felt the breeze pick up and a chill rolled through his body. This would be the first serious storm they'd been in since they joined the ship and he wasn't sure what to expect. He couldn't help but look at the clouds every time the lightning flashed. He watched as it came closer and closer. Soon it started to rain and Henry felt himself becoming soaked by freezing water quickly. He looked up at the crow's nest as Christopher and Cale came down. Then he at the captain standing on the top deck with Tolls. "*What will they do?*" He wondered as he and Christopher were ordered below decks.

"Turn our back to the storm. There's no outrunning it. We'll have to run with it until we can get out of it. I won't have the ship rolled in our attempt to get past it. It's here," the captain yelled to Tolls, "Try to steer us out whenever you can. Maybe we can get out of it faster if we steer west while we run with it south."

"Yes, sir," Tolls turned the helm until they were facing south.

∞∞∞

The storm raged above their heads as they sat waiting for orders. Only a few men were allowed on deck to work during the storm. They harnessed themselves and the ship in case they were swept overboard.

Henry's foot bounced nervously and he looked at Christopher to see how he was handling the tension. Christopher looked at Henry gravely.

Suddenly the fear seized Henry like a strong hand around his throat, and he realized he didn't want to die! He hadn't sailed the world like they had dreamed of as children! He hadn't made his fortune as a pirate! He'd never fallen in love! Then there was his family. He often thought of how he'd like to go home someday and see his mother. Maybe take her and Joanna something pretty from his travels. Would he make it out of this storm to do any of those things he had long dreamed of doing?

Henry watched as one of the men wretched into a bucket from the nausea of the tossing ship. It felt like the ship would be dashed to bits by the waves at any moment! They heaved up and down in the waves so steeply he wondered how they weren't all dead yet! Surely there would be no one left on the upper decks after this!

Henry wasn't sure when the ship stopped heaving, but he suddenly realized he could keep his balance. He stood as everyone else did and Robert opened the door to go up on deck. The men followed him out to a night sky with twinkling stars. They had broken through the storm and they could see it moving away from them.

Robert ran up the stairs to the top deck where he found Tolls clinging to the helm with white knuckles.

"You did it," Robert said with a soft slap on the quartermaster's shoulder.

Tolls blinked through the water that dripped down his face.

"The captain," Tolls said with a rough voice, "We lost the captain."

Robert looked at Tolls with shock.

"He wasn't tied to the ship?!"

"A wave crashed on us unexpectedly before he, our two helmsmen, and I could tie on. The wave took them overboard. I was able to hang on and tie myself onto the helm after the wave was gone," Tolls slowly loosened his grip on the helm.

"Chris," Robert called to the man who was helping a wounded sailor.

Christopher ran up the stairs to Robert.

"Take the helm while I get Captain Tolls below. I'll be right back."

Christopher looked at Tolls with surprise and then went to the helm to take hold as Robert put Tolls' arm around his shoulder. He watched as Robert helped Tolls down to the captain's cabin. He looked over the ship from the high-top deck. Watching as men helped those wounded from the storm. One was unconscious, another had a broken arm, and another had a bump on the head that looked like a coconut. Everyone was waterlogged and exhausted. Those who were unharmed worked to repair the ship enough to sail.

"With the missing sailors and more wounded, you'll have to step up and help with other jobs on the ship," Robert said as he came back on the top deck, "I've been watching you and I've noticed how quickly you pick things up. How about becoming my new helmsman? Both of the helmsmen were washed overboard. Do you think you and Henry could learn the job?"

"Yes, sir, I know we can."

"Good, I'll teach you, and you'll teach Henry. Starting now."

Robert spent the next half hour teaching Christopher enough to know how to start sailing toward their destination as the men below finished patching the ship.

"I'll show you more but I have a lot to do until the captain can take command," Robert said tiredly, "Just keep us on course for now."

"Yes, sir."

Christopher found the time at the helm peaceful and he felt connected to the ship in a whole new way. It made him feel bigger and more powerful somehow. When Robert sent Henry to him, he showed his friend what Robert had told him and Henry grinned.

"What?" Christopher shook his head in amusement at his friend.

"This sure beats swabbing the decks."

"It does," Christopher agreed.

They watched as men worked, and Robert soon joined them to show them how to adjust their course. They listened closely to all Robert said and then Christopher turned the helm to adjust their course. Soon Henry and Robert left, and he was alone on the top deck, staring into the starlit sky horizon.

"Drop anchor," Quartermaster Robert yelled to the crew as they came to the dock. "Good work, Chris," he said to the young man at the helm, "You've learned everything quickly and you've been a big help. Tonight, you have a drink on me."

"Thank you, sir."

"And tell Henry he's invited too. I know a good place."

"Yes, sir."

"Also, pass the word that everyone gets the night off. We've earned it."

"Yes, sir."

Christopher nodded and then went quickly down the stairs, telling the orders to every sailor he went past. He found Henry below helping the cook with cleaning up.

"We have the night off tonight," Christopher said as he walked up to them, "Robert has invited us to have a drink with him tonight."

Henry grinned, "That sounds good. I could use one after

the crossing we went through."

"We'll meet on the upper deck to follow him."

"Alright," Henry winked at Christopher, "Maybe he knows another girl you can fall for."

Christopher reached out and punched Henry's shoulder playfully.

"Maybe he knows one for you," Christopher smirked.

"Well, I hope so. I don't think it'd be fair if you're the only one who gets any girls."

That evening as they followed Robert and Cale off the ship they all seemed to have a lighter step.

"I hope you boys like lamb. This place is the best in the world for perfectly roasted lamb." Robert led the way through the crowded streets of Charleston.

"I've eaten there plenty of times, but I don't know if I'd go as far as saying they are the best in the world," Cale said as they walked.

"To each their own," Robert said without looking back at Cale.

They spent the evening drinking and eating what Henry and Christopher agreed was some of the best roast lamb they ever had. The barmaid flirted with Christopher and brought them free rounds of ale.

They were so involved with the drama playing out between Christopher and the barmaid, they didn't notice the three surly men watching from across the tavern.

∞∞∞

The Maria sailed towards Florida slowly. Not all the repairs had been done to the extent Captain Tolls needed, but the storm had put them behind in getting their shipment to its destination. He decided they would get the repairs done in Florida. But they were forced to sail slowly to keep from causing more damage to the ship. The storm had put a small hole in the side, thankfully above the water line, but it meant bailing water out of the ship as the waves reached the hole. A detail that Henry and Christopher found themselves on when they weren't at the helm.

A day had passed when the call came from the crow's nest. A ship had been spotted behind them and it was gaining quickly.

"Pirates," Tolls growled, "They'll overtake us."

"What should we do?" Robert asked as he looked at the ship through a spyglass.

"We're in no condition to fight them, and if we surrender they may let us live. But tell the men to arm themselves just in case. Then roll up the sails and put up a white flag."

"Yes, sir."

Robert did as he was ordered and the men scrambled to arm themselves. The thrill of meeting real pirates for the first time excited Henry and Christopher, though they tried not to show it to their fellow crewmen, who looked nervous.

"Men, if you ever want to go home or become respectable men again, you'll find a new name. Understand?" Robert said to Christopher and Henry as they walked towards their place in line on the upper deck.

"Yes, sir," Henry said as Christopher gave a short nod.

The entire crew stood on the deck watching as the pirate ship overtook them and pulled alongside.

Across from them, they saw a grinning, motley crew of pirates who looked like they came from hell itself. All held swords at the ready, and when the ship stopped alongside them, the pirates boarded the Maria like hell hounds after prey.

Christopher stood firmly in his place and didn't flinch as a scruffy pirate got close to his face and chuckled before moving on to Henry. Christopher tried not to flinch at the stench of the man's breath! It smelled of rotting meat!

"Now, which one of you bloody honest sailor boys is the captain?" said a tall man with a scraggly red beard and red hair sticking out of his hat. The feather in his hat stood up like a proud peacock spreading its wings. His face sagged slightly on one side and a scar ran from his right ear to the left side of his chin.

Tolls stepped forward, "I am."

The man walked over to stand in front of Tolls thoughtfully.

"Well, there can only be one captain at a time. And I'm it."

The man took out his sword and sliced Tolls' head off with one blow! Tolls' head fell to the deck with a thud! Christopher pulled himself together quickly and looked straight ahead to not show fear. He remembered Henry and looked at him quickly to make sure he wasn't showing fear either. Henry was looking straight ahead as well, but his lips were pressed so tightly together that they turned white.

"I'm Captain Brambell. You've all just become my pirates and will work for me. We heard your ship was on its way to Florida with a shipment of goods, but having a hard time after a store. We came to offer aid like the good friends we are. This ship will continue on its journey and continue working like a good merchant ship. The only difference is that you will bring your profits to me each time you make one. Your new captain will be my most trusted first mate, Matthew the Hunter. You'll have some crewmen from my own ship to help replace some that you lost. They will make sure you turn pirate-like proper." He looked at the crew of the Maria darkly. "Would anyone like to be dropped off at the nearest port instead of becoming a pirate?"

The new man they had taken on at Charleston stepped forward nervously.

"Please, sir, I have a family."

Captain Brambell walked over to the man with an evil smile and Christopher braced himself for what was coming. The captain stopped in front of the man and put a hand on the man's shoulder.

"It's alright son. If your family is willing to let you go sailing, then they probably don't need you as much as you think."

Suddenly the captain's sword ran through the man's middle and out the other side! The poor man gagged and fell off the sword to the deck. The captain stood over the man and ran his sword into him again, and again until the man stopped moving.

Henry bit his lip with fear until he felt blood in his mouth. He knew Christopher would tell him not to show fear, but he wasn't sure if he was succeeding.

The captain stepped back and walked over to a barrel of seawater they used for swabbing the decks, and dipped his sword into it to clean it off.

"Anyone else?" The captain asked loudly.

No one moved a muscle.

"Good. I'll leave you to First Mate Hunter." With that, the captain crossed a plank to the other ship.

Henry took a small shaky breath until he saw the first mate step forward.

"Who's been second on this ship until now?" the man asked. His brown hair was pulled back smartly in a ponytail as he took off his hat. He threw the hat to another pirate behind him. The pirate caught it and put it on his own head. Then Hunter reached down and took the hat off the severed head of Captain Tolls, and put the hat on his head.

Robert stepped forward.

"I'm the quartermaster, sir."

"Well now you're my first mate," Hunter said, "Your first order of business is to get us underway, with the help of your new crewmen. There's ten of them and they are more than willing to help." He slapped the shoulder of the man he gave his hat to and the man grinned. "This is your new boatswain, Mr. Timmy the Stretch. Mr. Stretch will see to it that everyone does their job according to the pirate code. If you're unfamiliar with these codes I just so happen to have a copy right here." He took out a rolled-up parchment from inside his vest and unrolled it with a serious look. "You'll read it or have someone read it for you. Sign it. I'll proudly hang it in my cabin and if you break one I'll show you which one you broke before you die." He handed the paper to Mr. Stretch.

Hunter walked along in front of the crew looking them over. Then he walked back and nodded to Robert. Robert turned towards the crew and barked out orders to sign the code. The men scrambled to do as ordered.

"Don't sign your names. Just put an X," Robert whispered to Henry and Christopher when Hunter was walking away. They nodded their understanding and did what he said.

Captain Hunter went to the top deck and looked around while the men finished signing the paper. Robert went up to stand beside him like a good first mate would.

"What's your name sailor?" Captain Hunter asked him.

"Cob, sir," Robert answered.

"Mr. Cob, get us underway and on the same heading as before."

"Yes, sir," Robert started yelling orders for the men to get underway.

Christopher took the helm, and Henry was forced to throw the dead bodies overboard. Then a mop was pressed in his hand and he used the seawater to clean the deck. Christopher watched Henry as he gripped the helm tighter than he needed to. They had finally become what they had talked about since they were boys. They were pirates. But instead of the thrill they had been feeling earlier, he felt a little unsure as he thought of Tolls' body and head being thrown overboard.

Chapter 6

They finally limped into a port in Florida and unloaded the cargo. The original crew of the Maria wasn't allowed shore leave in case they had any ideas of trying to abandon the ship. The pirates who had come aboard went ashore to celebrate their newly acquired vessel.

"I say we overpower the captain and his man while the rest of the crew are gone. We can easily get rid of them and get out of here. We'll pick up another shipment of cargo somewhere else."

"Don't be a fool, Brack," Robert said quietly before taking another bite of ration.

They were sitting with Cale, Christopher, and Henry on the lower deck.

"If you didn't succeed you'd be a dead man. Besides, it's not so bad. We aren't doing anything different than we were before," Christopher said firmly.

"Except now if we're caught we'll hang as pirates," Brack grumbled.

"Relax, Brack," Robert said sternly, "Don't make things worse. No one is going to know we're pirates as long as we're running like a regular merchant ship."

Brack shook his head.

"Everyone just operate like normal, and don't disrupt the balance," Robert ordered with a stern look to each of them.

"Yes, sir," Christopher said quietly.

"Sounds to me like you have some doubts about our good captain's abilities."

They all turned towards the door and watched as the

boatswain walked in with an evil grin on his face.

"No, sir, Mr. Stretch," Henry spoke up nervously as they all stood, "We have full confidence in the captain, and we are happy to have him."

"Calm down," Christopher whispered to Henry.

Stretch walked towards Brack and stood in front of him.

"How would you like the chance to tell the captain your complaints? I think he'd enjoy hearing them."

Brack looked at Stretch nervously and shook his head.

"No, sir, I didn't mean anything by what I said."

Stretch put his face in front of Brack's.

"Too late," Stretch said quietly with glee.

Then Stretch grabbed Brack by the head and dragged him up the stairs. They all followed them with concern. Stretch yelled to the captain, who came out of his cabin at the commotion.

"Good Captain, I thought you'd like to hear this sorry creature's complaints yourself, sir."

"Complaints, Mr. Stretch?" The captain walked down to the deck and stood in front of Brack, "You're upset about something, sir?"

"No, sir," Brack said nervously.

"He was talking mutiny, sir," Stretch offered up.

"Mutiny? Well, that just won't do, will it, Mr. Stretch?"

"No, sir, what should we do about it, Captain?"

The captain wiggled his finger for them to follow him down to the lower deck and everyone obeyed. The captain led them down to the hold and opened barrel lids until he found one that was half empty of water. He stepped back and held the lid as he pointed to the barrel.

"I think this will do Mr. Stretch."

"I like it, Captain, but may I ask for someone else to do the honors? I don't fancy getting wet before I go out celebrating. My watch is almost up."

"Of course, Mr. Stretch," the captain pointed at Henry and Christopher, "Put this sod in the barrel and nail it shut."

Henry and Christopher looked at each other in horror and then at Brack.

"Do it, or I'll find barrels for each of you as his conspirators," the captain ordered with a menacing look.

"Yes, sir," Christopher said quietly.

He and Henry walked over to Brack and pulled him towards the barrel as Brack protested and begged. They got him in the barrel and the captain put the lid on. Henry held the lid down as Christopher nailed it shut. They could hear Brack yelling through the barrel, and they looked at each other before turning to the captain, who was smiling at them.

"Now see? Proper pirates follow orders. You both just showed him how to be proper pirates. He stays in the barrel until I say otherwise. We can't have him making trouble for us while we're in port." The captain turned on his heel and walked away; back up to the upper deck. The other men followed, leaving Christopher and Henry alone in the room with the barrel.

Henry stared at the barrel, and Christopher stared at Henry.

"We can't help him now. He brought this on himself." Christopher said quietly as he stepped close to Henry. "Come on, let's go back to the bunk room."

Henry shook his head, "But we did this to him. We put him in there. What if he dies? His blood will be on our hands."

"What did you think pirates do, Henry? They aren't kittens. This is what we wanted, and now we have it. Get over it and move on. We didn't do anything to Brack. It's the captain's doing," He made his voice stern, "Now get out, Henry."

Christopher gave his friend a shove towards the door of the hold and followed without a look back.

They were barely out of port when the captain ordered

Christopher and Henry to bring the barrel, with Brack inside, to the upper deck. The crew was assembled to face the captain standing on the top deck.

"If you have any more ideas about mutiny in your heads, I suggest you get rid of them. Talk of mutiny is not tolerated." The captain came down the steps and crossed over to look at Christopher and Henry, "What are your names?"

"James, sir," Christopher said without blinking.

"Liam, sir," Henry said.

"James and Liam here have shown themselves to be proper pirates who take orders. They will demonstrate what pirates look like so the rest of you know," the captain stepped back, "Throw the barrel overboard."

Henry looked at Christopher with wide eyes, but Christopher didn't look at Henry. Instead, he stepped towards the barrel and waited for Henry to join him. Henry slowly stepped to the barrel and they picked it up. They walked to the edge of the ship and looked over the side before looking at each other.

In that moment they silently acknowledged there was no coming back from what they were about to do.

Then they tipped the barrel, with Brack inside, over the side of the ship.

They turned to look at the captain who was smiling at them.

"Good," Then the captain's face turned dark, "Now get back to work you scums, and I don't ever want to hear of mutiny again."

Henry watched with an expressionless face as the captain went back up to his cabin.

"Liam..."

Christopher stepped close, but Henry shook his head and walked away towards the stairs, where he climbed them and took his place at the helm.

∞∞∞

Christopher had never seen Henry so serious. His grin hadn't been seen since they had become pirates, and Christopher didn't blame him. There wasn't much to smile about. Things were tense on the ship, and there was nothing good about it.

One day Christopher figured out where they were going and when Henry came to relieve him of duty, he pulled Henry close so no one could hear.

"I know where we're going. Carolsport."

"What?" Henry looked at him with surprise.

"I overheard the captain and Robert studying the map and they let out where we're going," he looked at Henry seriously, "If you want I'll make some excuse, like your death, and you can go home."

Henry looked at him in shock, "Why would I do that?"

"Look, this hasn't turned out like you thought. I know that, and I want you to go home if you want to."

"What would I do in Carolsport?"

"I don't know, but I'm sure you'll find something," Christopher stepped back as he saw Robert walk up the steps, "Just think about it."

"I don't need to think about it. I'm staying," Henry said as he took the helm, "I can still see them even if I can't stay."

"Fine, but if you change your mind, I'll understand," Christopher walked away.

Henry thought about home. What would it be like? Would they be glad to see him or would his father bar him from their home? Surely Mother wouldn't let him do that. Henry couldn't help the smile that came to his face as he thought of her.

∞∞∞

"You have three days of leave after the cargo is unloaded. The new cargo won't be ready for several days," Robert looked at Henry and Christopher seriously, "Be back to the ship on time or the captain will have your hide."

"Yes, sir," Henry said with a grin.

"What are you so happy about?" Robert asked with a frown.

"Just glad to get off the ship, sir," Christopher said as he put his hand on Henry's shoulder, and pulled on him to walk towards the edge of the ship.

Henry could have run off the ship and towards home, but Christopher held him in check. They didn't want anyone to know they were in their hometown. Especially not the captain or the pirates that came with him, so they walked the streets calmly. When they came in view of Henry's house he stopped and just stared at it.

"What's wrong?" Christopher asked.

"I'm not sure if I should go," Henry said calmly as he stared at the house.

"Why wouldn't you?"

"What if they don't want me around? We are pirates now after all."

"They don't know that," Christopher pushed Henry's back to make him start walking.

They were almost to the house when Henry's mother came out of the house with a basket. The sight of her was all it took and Henry picked up his pace.

"Mother!" he called to her, and she looked up at him in shock.

Then she dropped the basket and ran to him. He embraced her tightly and swallowed the emotion he felt as he did.

"Oh, my Henry!" his mother started crying and then looked up at his face with a joyful smile, "Oh, Henry! You came home."

"We did," he answered with a pang of guilt.

"We?" she looked behind him and saw Christopher.

Christopher nodded and turned to walk away.

"Christopher! Don't you dare walk away from me!" she yelled at him.

Surprised by her sternness, he turned to look at her. She waved at him to come to her, so he did. She embraced him like the only mother he'd ever had, and a tiny pang of guilt hit him suddenly.

"Hello, Mrs. Johnson," he said respectfully.

She released him and looked at them both with eyes full of love.

"My how you've both grown. Such strong young men you've become. And you had your birthdays while you were away. I missed making you each a special dinner. Come in, and I'll make you something to eat," she took each of their hands and pulled them towards the door of the house.

They followed her in and she made them sit at the table.

"Your father will be home from the church any time, and Joanna should be home soon. I can't wait for them to see you both." She chatted as she got them each some butter and bread, "Now eat what you want, but don't spoil your appetite for supper. I made a roast that I was worried would be too big for the three of us, but it's just right for the five of us."

"Oh, I wasn't planning to stay. I just walked Henry over," Christopher said as he tried to stand, but she pushed him back down.

"Of course, you're staying. You're a part of this family too. I've missed you both. How dare you two run off and only leave a note. You could have at least hugged me goodbye," she scolded them before going to the fireplace to check on the roast.

Christopher looked at Henry, and Henry grinned at him. Christopher shook his head and smiled a little.

The door opened and Joanna stepped into the house.

"Mother, why is your basket..." she stopped short when she saw Christopher and Henry.

"Well, don't just stand there staring at them silly girl. Hug your brother," Mrs. Johnson said with a smile.

Joanna could feel a tear fall down her cheek as she stared at Christopher. She thought she'd never see him again. After they had been gone a month, she realized it wasn't just Henry she missed. She had dreamed about the day she might see Christopher again, but she hadn't held out much hope.

Henry stood and came to her and hugged her. She hugged him back but she couldn't keep her eyes from Christopher. She wanted to go to him and wrap her arms around him but she hesitated with uncertainty.

"So you've come back."

They all looked at the open doorway to see Pastor Johnson standing there looking at Christopher and Henry.

Henry stared at his father with uncertainty. They just stood staring at each other for a time and everyone waited quietly.

The pastor finally moved to put his things down on a nearby chair and then to the table where he sat. No one moved at first as they all looked at him with surprise. Slowly Mrs. Johnson started to put supper on the table and Joanna went to help her. Henry sat back down next to Christopher.

"So you ran off to become sailors," the pastor stated more than asked.

"Yes, sir," Henry replied quietly.

"And you've come home for what?"

"We're in port for a few days, and we wanted to see you," Henry watched his father talk without expression, making it hard to tell what he was thinking.

"Is this how it is to be then? We see you whenever you're in port."

"I'm afraid we have no control over where we go, sir. We just got lucky this time," Henry said with a slight shrug.

"Or it was God's will for you to come home to see the family you so rudely ran out on," his father's voice went up just a little, and Henry could tell he was upset.

Henry didn't say anything because he knew his answer wouldn't be what his father wanted to hear. Henry doubted very much that God had anything to do with it.

"Have you seen your father yet, Christopher?" the pastor asked.

Christopher looked up with shock. Wasn't his father dead?! He had killed him before they left!

"My father?"

"Yes, I just saw him in town. He didn't say anything about you so I assume you haven't been home."

"No, sir," Christopher's jaw set sternly, "I don't care to see my father."

"You should. He's not been the same since you left."

"What do you mean," Christopher asked, confused.

"He's been in church every Sabbath since you left. He hasn't had a drink since either. He said he blamed himself over you leaving."

Christopher couldn't believe what he was hearing! The pastor must be talking about someone else because it didn't sound like his father at all.

"I still have no intention of seeing him," Christopher said firmly.

Mrs. Johnson and Joanna finished setting the food on the table and sat down.

"But you'll come to my home and pretend to be a part of my family as always," the pastor said irritably.

Christopher glared at the man darkly while Mrs. Johnson and Joanna protested on his behalf.

"I don't mean to be in your way. Like I told Mrs. Johnson, I just came to walk Henry home. I'll leave," Christopher stood and the protest from the females grew louder and surprisingly angry. He couldn't help but look at them and see their angry faces turned towards the pastor.

"Thomas, don't you dare send him away. I just got him back," Mrs. Johnson said with a frown at the pastor. Then she looked at Christopher sternly, "You'll sit back down and eat with us, and I won't have any more such talk at my table. Now sit," she ordered.

Christopher wanted to obey, but he wasn't going to spend the evening being insulted when he could be at the tavern drinking instead.

"Sit," the pastor ordered, "I can't have you making my dear wife cry like you did the last time you left."

Christopher felt a little pang of guilt at the idea he had made her cry, so he slowly sat back down.

The pastor prayed for the meal and Mrs. Johnson filled their plates for them.

"Am I right to assume you won't be staying long?" the pastor asked without looking up from his plate.

Christopher looked at Henry, and Henry at him.

"Yes, Father, we leave in a few days."

"Oh, Henry, I wish you would stay," his mother said softly.

"I'm sorry, but I can't."

Everyone fell silent and no one ate much except the pastor who hadn't lost his appetite at all.

"I'm sure Henry can write to you," Christopher broke the silence.

Mrs. Johnson smiled a little, "I'd like that."

"And you will write also, Chris?" Joanna's question came softly but slightly demanding.

Christopher looked at her with surprise. Her face showed earnest interest in her command. She was clearly not asking. She wanted him to write. He studied her a moment. Her back was rigidly straight with purpose. She may be of an average stature but she had always seemed small to him. Now though as he took in her womanly features he realized he had failed to notice that she was no longer Henry's sister who followed them everywhere she was able. She was truly a woman in her own right. Her beauty had become enchanting with her black raven hair falling from her bun, into her mesmerizing violet eyes. But it was her commanding tone that made him realize she had truly become a woman

Movement from her father next to him brought him out of the trance he'd found himself in.

"I'm afraid I'm not much of a writer," he glanced at her father, who Christopher was sure didn't want them writing to each other. The man glared at Christopher like he had read every thought that had flashed through Christopher's mind about Joanna.

"Oh, I don't think that's true." Joanna's voice commanded his attention back to her and he obliged. "You never had problems with your letters to the girls in school. Surely it's easier to write your own family."

Her cold sarcasm about his letters to the girls at school made him smirk.

"I didn't realize my letters were public knowledge," he took a drink of water as he held her gaze over the rim of his cup.

"They were quite famous actually." Joanna looked annoyed now by a memory, "Jenny nearly gave me a paper cut waving hers in my face."

Christopher chuckled, "You mean the one where I asked if she would help me with writing my essay on pigs? Yes, quite the love letter." His chuckle turned into laughter.

Joanna rolled her eyes as Henry joined in.

"Did you want me to write you about pigs, Joanna?" Christopher meant it as a joke, but he had said it too softly and it came out sounding more like a proposal. He cleared his throat, "I'm afraid we have no pigs."

The table grew quiet and Joanna stared at him with something like longing.

"It doesn't have to be pigs." She almost whispered it.

"What places have you been to?" Mrs. Johnson asked quickly to change the subject.

That was all Henry needed to start a long story about their adventures, leaving out the part of becoming pirates.

When the evening ended the women worked on washing and putting away the dishes, and the pastor went to the sitting room.

"I'm going to go show my face at the tavern so the crew doesn't grow suspicious. I'll cover for you while you stay with your family for the next couple of days," Christopher said quietly to Henry.

"You could stay," Henry frowned.

Christopher smirked, "I don't think your father would like that very much."

"No, but mother would."

Christopher's smirk grew, "I bet Joanna would."

Henry's light mood went dark fast, "Don't even think about Joanna like that."

Christopher shook his head in amusement, "Why? She's pretty..."

"Because I know what you are now, and I have no intention of letting my sister fall for a pirate," Henry said gruffly with anger coming to his eyes, "Don't forget I was around for Sophie too."

Christopher grew serious, "If I didn't know better I'd think you hate me as much as your father."

Henry relaxed and shook his head slowly, "No, not at all, Chris. I just want better for my sister than us." Henry looked down at the ground and then back up at Christopher, "I could never hate you, Chris. You're my brother."

Christopher relaxed and nodded, "Same here. I won't hurt Joanna."

"Thanks," Henry said, relieved.

Then Christopher smirked as he stepped towards the kitchen, "But that doesn't mean I don't like her."

Henry looked at him sharply as he walked away.

"I have to be going," Christopher said to the women.

"Already?" Mrs. Johnson said with sadness, "Why don't you stay here tonight, Christopher."

"I'm sorry but I'm needed elsewhere."

"You'll be back tomorrow though right?" she looked at him sternly.

"I'll come for supper."

Her smile blossomed across her face, and she reached up to kiss his cheek, "You're such a good boy. I'll make your favorite, shephards pie tomorrow. Don't be late."

"Yes, ma'am," he turned to look at Joanna and he could see her beautiful violet eyes staring into his soul. He stepped towards her and lifted her hand to his lips with a soft kiss pressed to her palm. He lowered his tone, "Good night, Joanna."

"Good night, Chris," she said softly with a small smile.

He turned away to walk towards the door and looked at Henry with a goading smirk. Henry glared at him in return. Christopher stopped next to Henry and whispered.

"They shouldn't tell anyone we're here. We don't want it to get back to the ship."

Henry grunted, "Alright."

Christopher left and Henry let out a breath of anger. He flexed the fingers of his hand trying to calm down. If Christopher left Joanna in the state he left Sophie... Henry wasn't sure what he would do.

When Joanna and his mother were finished putting away supper, Henry followed them to the sitting room where he found his father.

Henry stopped in the doorway and cleared his throat a little.

"I need to ask you all to keep our return quiet." His family looked at him with confusion and concern. "Sailors aren't supposed to tell one another where they are from in case someone turns pirate and uses it against you." He shrugged nonchalantly, "It's not a big deal, it's just a safety precaution."

"Care for a game of chess, father?" Henry asked as he set in a hair near the chess board.

"No, I don't care for a game of chess with my runaway son. You can't just come home, Henry, and expect life to be the way you left it. It's not fair to the ones who love you. If you want to be a part of this family, then do so." his father spoke gruffly and Henry wasn't sure what he meant.

"What do you mean if I want to be a part? I can't stay,

father."

"Then while you're here you'll live by my rules if you're to stay in my house. Starting with nightly bible reading."

His father picked up his Bible from a small table, and handed it to Henry. Henry stared at the book leerily. He'd read from the book before, but he never cared enough about what he read to try and understand it. He had no use for it either. The Bible was always judging you about whether or not you were a saint. He was no saint. Throwing Brack overboard alive was proof of that.

But he loved his family and wanted to spend time with them while he could, so he took the Bible.

"Where?"

"Luke, chapter 15. Verse 11 through 32," his father said firmly.

Henry turned to find the reference and began reading. It was a story he remembered reading once before, and he tried not to sound sarcastic as he read the story of the prodigal son. When he finished he closed the book and held it out to his father. His father took it with a stern look at Henry.

"Did you listen to the message?"

"I understand your meaning," Henry said wryly, "Now can we play chess?"

His father looked at him with doubt, but relented with a nod.

Chapter 7

Christopher walked along the road to the tavern thoughtfully. He had been goading Henry about Joanna, but if he was serious he couldn't say he wasn't drawn to her. She had always been beautiful, but just in the months they'd been gone, she seemed to have grown into an exquisite woman.

He walked into Mr. Brown's tavern and found Robert and Cale sitting at a table.

"Where have you been?" Cale asked as Christopher sat down, "Where's...Liam?"

Christopher looked around at the drunken pirates and sailors and leaned closer to Robert and Cale.

"You know this is where you picked us up at?"

Robert nodded.

"This is our hometown. Hen...Liam went to see his parents and sister."

Robert and Cale looked at him like he had grown tentacles.

"Do you know how dangerous that is? If anyone found out who you are you'd never be safe here," Robert said quietly, "You should have both stayed on the ship."

Christopher shrugged as Mr. Brown came over with a mug and pitcher of ale, and set it in front of him. Christopher didn't make eye contact with him in hopes Mr. Brown wouldn't recognize him. Thankfully, someone dropped a mug of ale on the floor, distracting Mr. Brown.

"So where were you?" Robert asked quietly, "Visiting your family too?"

Christopher took a long drink before answering.

"I was with Liam's."

Before any more could be said, someone pulled the fourth chair from the table and sat down with a bottle in his hand.

"You lot need something stronger than ale," he slammed the bottle on the table hard enough to slosh the liquid out of it.

Christopher smirked at the man who ran a hand through his oily black hair and pursed his lips as he brought the bottle to them.

"What are you drinking, Pierre?" Christopher asked the man as the bottle hit the table again.

Pierre grinned, "Rum."

"Can't say I've ever had that," Christopher said.

Pierre waved the bottle in front of Christopher's face. Christopher grabbed the bottle and took a drink. Then he nearly spit it all out on the floor from the strong taste and slight burn he wasn't expecting.

Christopher immediately coughed, nearly spitting out the rum. It had a strong flavor and burned his throat.

Pierre laughed like it was the funniest thing he'd ever seen.

"Such a boy you are. Never had rum," Pierre laughed some more.

Christopher glared at Robert and Cale as they laughed too. Then he reached for the bottle and took another swig.

This time he was expecting the burn and strong taste, so he drank slower. It worked and he didn't spit it out. This earned him a little more respect. When Pierre reached for it Christopher held it away from him.

"No, I think since you laughed at me, I should drink the rest myself."

Pierre laughed again and waved at a barmaid, "Bring me another bottle of rum."

∞∞∞

"Hello, big man."

Cale's voice sounded overly loud and it rang inside Christopher's head. His head felt like he had been beaten on the head with one of his father's bottles. He opened his eyes and found Cale looking down at him.

"Cob says he thinks you should stay on board tonight instead of getting yourself into trouble."

"What? Who?" Christopher willed his head to clear from the fog so he could understand what Cale was saying. He slowly sat up and Cale handed him a drink of water.

Cale leaned closer.

"Robert said to stay on board the ship so you don't get into trouble."

"Why would I get into trouble?"

"James, my boy, you are a very fun companion with a couple of swigs of rum, but you're dangerous with a bottle of the stuff in you. It was all we could do to get you back here last night without you giving away everything. No more rum for you boy."

"I can't stay. I made a promise to be somewhere tonight."

"If it's what I think you're going to say then I suggest you don't. That's just as dangerous, and not just for you. I can't keep you here, but just promise you won't drink any more rum for a while."

"Don't worry. I have no intention of drinking any more rum, tonight."

Christopher walked towards the house and still felt a slight headache. He shook his head at himself. He'd been foolish. He'd lost control. He had to be in control! There was too much at stake! Especially here with people they cared about, and this wasn't a time for mistakes.

He was almost to the house when Joanna walked outside

with a basket and walk around the side of the house. He followed her to where she was taking the clothes off the line.

"Hello," he said pleasantly.

Joanna was startled but smiled as soon as she saw him.

"Hello," she walked closer to him, "I'm glad you came back."

"I promised your mother I would," he looked at the clothes, "May I help?"

Joanna looked at him like he'd said he'd jump off a cliff.

"You want to help me with clothes? Don't you consider that a woman's job?" she smirked and her violet eyes twinkled with amusement.

"I was just trying to be a gentleman," he said with a smile.

Joanna gave a soft laugh.

"You're no gentleman, Christopher Lavin," she teased.

Christopher grinned, "Minx, what do you know? Maybe I am."

Joanna laughed again, "You're more likely a pirate."

This made Christopher grow cold and his smile turned into an intense stare with slight fear that she might know the truth.

Joanna looked at him with surprise at his serious manner that came so suddenly.

"What's wrong?" she asked with a slight frown.

Christopher shook his head and made his smile return, but it didn't reach his eyes.

"Let me help you fold these sheets," he said changing the subject and walking towards the line.

She followed him and they folded several sheets before going inside.

Christopher walked in to find Henry sitting at the table talking to his mother while she worked. He looked over and glared at Christopher when he saw the basket in his arms. Christopher smirked and gave Henry a wink. Henry's glare grew darker and his jaw set angrily. Christopher put the basket down on a chair and sat down next to Henry.

Henry leaned over to whisper, “Chris, I swear if you hurt Joanna like you did Sophie I’ll kill you myself.”

Christopher looked at Henry seriously, “I can’t help that she seems to like me.”

“You don’t need to make her think you return it.”

“What if I do? What if I like her more than you think?” Christopher shrugged.

“Like her enough to stay?”

“Like her enough to write to her if she wants me to.”

Henry shook his head in exasperation, “We don’t know if we’ll ever be back here. You can’t promise her anything like a future. Let her go.”

Christopher looked at Joanna thoughtfully but didn’t respond.

Before they could continue their debate, Pastor Johnson walked in and joined them for supper. When they finished, Mrs. Johnson made Christopher promise to return the next evening for supper. Christopher promised and made his way back to the ship.

“Henry,” Joanna moved to sit next to him at the table as their mother went to the sitting room, “Did you become pirates?”

Henry looked at her startled, “What? Why would you ask that?”

“Because I was teasing Chris about it earlier and he became very serious. He almost seemed upset that I called him a pirate,” she looked at him suspiciously.

Henry looked at her sternly for a moment.

“Yes, we didn’t have a choice. Our ship was forced into the service of a pirate. We run like a merchant ship, but that’s why I said that you can’t tell anyone we’re here. We don’t want it to get back to our ship who we are in truth. If they found out they could use it against us. We’d never be able to come home again without the threat of hanging.”

She looked at him with wide eyes, “Henry, you should get

out before you're named a pirate."

"We aren't using our real names, and we don't exactly have the freedom to abandon ship. We had to sign articles that said we belonged to the ship. Desertion will get us killed if we're found."

Tears threatened to spill down her cheeks, "But if you aren't using your real names then you should be able to get off and hide until they're gone."

"Honestly, Joanna, we don't want to get off," he looked at her sympathetically as she stared at him with betrayal that he wouldn't want to get away from the ship, "I'm sorry, Joanna."

"Chris doesn't want to leave either?" she asked sadly.

"No," Henry said firmly as he silently cursed his friend for making her upset, "Please don't ask anymore."

She nodded slightly and rose to walk to the sitting room.

He watched her walk away and a small stab of guilt hit him for hurting her.

∞∞∞

The next morning, Christopher walked towards the home he had hated his whole life. He wanted to see if it was true. If his father was alive.

He stopped at the front door to take a breath before knocking. Christopher grew surprised at the sight of the man standing before him. Clean-shaven with hair neatly combed. The man before him was so unlike the man he knew.

His father smiled in delight at the sight of him, "Would you come in, son?"

Christopher followed his father into the house slowly. The house was different too. The broken chair that had sat in the sitting room since the day his father threw it at him, was gone. There weren't any bottles on the floor, and the house was neat and clean.

He stopped at the horrifying closet his father had locked him in too many times to count. The memories came flooding back, and he felt himself grow stiff with hatred.

"Son?"

Christopher looked at his father, who was standing in the kitchen. Fresh bread sat on the table with some butter and his father smiled at him.

"Please, sit."

Christopher took a few more steps toward the table but remained standing.

"I can't stay. I just wanted to see if you were truly still alive. I thought I had killed you the morning I left."

"Well, I blacked out and woke to find blood on my face. It terrified me and I started to remember what happened. When I realized you were gone after a few days, I went to the pastor's home to look for you. Then I found out Henry was gone and you along with him. Guilt and shame at realizing I'd driven you away started to eat at me. I haven't had a drop to drink since you left. I started going to church and found myself yearning to learn more about God. God saved me through you, son. Thank you."

Christopher's eyes narrowed, and he shook his head, "I don't believe you."

"I know it's hard to believe. I was pretty bad to you, son. I'm sorry for all I did to you. You deserved better and I will never forgive myself. I hope someday you can, but I understand if you don't forgive me either."

"I don't. I never will," Christopher said darkly and his voice became angry from the hate he felt for the man before him, "I don't believe a word you've said. It's all a lie."

With that, he turned on his heel and walked out of the house.

∞∞∞

That evening Christopher showed up before supper and sat down at the table to wait as Mrs. Johnson and Joanna finished making supper.

"Did you tell them?" Christopher asked Henry.

Henry shook his head, "I haven't been able to yet."

"Tell us what, dear?" Mrs. Johnson asked from the fireplace.

Henry cleared his throat, "This is our last night. We leave tomorrow."

It was only a half lie. They would be leaving the Johnsons even though the ship didn't sail for another day. They wouldn't be allowed to leave the ship again after tonight though.

"We have to go back to the ship tonight," Henry tried to sound kind as he saw his mother's face go from surprise to sadness and tears pooled in her eyes.

Joanna couldn't stand what she had just heard. Tears fell from her eyes unchecked. Suddenly she found herself doing what she knew she'd regret later. She threw her arms around Christopher's neck and buried her head on his shoulder.

"I thought I'd never see you again," she said softly.

Christopher was shocked by her reaction. Something in him melted though, and he pulled her down onto his lap and put his arms around her. He wasn't sure how long they sat there with Henry and his mother watching in shock. Henry's look turned to a dark glare, but Christopher ignored it.

"Please don't leave me again," her voice was broken and soft tears could be heard in her words.

He felt like someone shoved a knife into his heart and he mentally pulled it out as he pushed her away slowly. She looked at him, begging him to stay. He pushed her till she was standing and then stood himself.

"I can't do that," he said sternly.

Christopher looked at Henry, "I'll be at the tavern if you need me."

Henry nodded.

"Please, Chris," Joanna grabbed his arm.

He gently grabbed her wrist and pulled her hand off his arm, "I can't stay here. There's no future for us. I'm a sailor and that's all I'll ever be."

Joanna took a breath and tried to calm down even though she just wanted to cry more. She'd do anything to keep him there, but what would he want with her when his adventures had just begun?

"I can't help the way I feel, Chris. I care too much for you. I'll wait for you no matter how long it takes," she said as firmly as she could manage.

"I don't want that for your life, Joanna. You should find someone who can give you a real life. Someone who will be here for you all the time. Not someone who is gone without knowing if he'll ever return."

"We can write."

"I'll never receive your letters," he said gently, "Move on with your life, Joanna."

"Never. I can't believe you don't care enough about me to at least write."

"Of course I care about you," He was getting irritated with her, and himself, for having let it come to this. But he couldn't deny he cared about her. Not in the same way he had Sophie. It was different. Deeper. He wanted to protect her. He'd stay if he wasn't in love with the sea more.

He stepped closer to her.

"How could I not care for you? I always have. Goodbye, Joanna," he said softly before kissing her forehead. Then he released her and went to Mrs. Johnson, and hugged her, "Thank you for caring for me. I should have said so sooner. You're the mother I never had. Thank you."

"I love you, my son," she said sweetly as she hugged him.

"Goodbye," he kissed her cheek and turned to leave.

He walked out of the door and stopped outside to take a breath.

The door opened behind him and he turned just as Joanna

flung herself into his arms and kissed him. Her lips were warm and he couldn't help but relent and kiss her in return.

"Joanna, I promised Henry I wouldn't hurt you," he said softly between kisses, and his hand moved behind her neck.

"You're not. Just promise to write to me, and I'll love you from a distance," her words came breathlessly.

He didn't respond and she suddenly reached up and grabbed his chin, and pulled back enough to see his face.

"Promise or I'll tell everyone you're a pirate."

He looked at her darkly.

"What?"

"You gave yourself away yesterday when I was teasing you about it. I know you and Henry too well. I asked Henry and he admitted it. Now promise you'll write to me," she said sternly, "I love you."

He stared at her a moment more before he answered softly, "I promise."

Then he kissed her again and felt himself intensify the kiss. He wanted nothing more than to kiss her forever. The idea of having to leave her hit him hard. He felt like someone had punched him and the emotion it brought stuck in his throat. He stopped the kiss and rested his head on hers.

"I'm sorry I can't stay, love."

"It's alright. I know you can't. Just promise to come back to me whenever you can."

"I promise I'll write," he kissed her softly again and then slowly released her, "Goodbye, love."

"Goodbye, Chris."

It was all he could do to walk away from her. Every fiber in his being wanted to stay and love her, but he knew he couldn't. It would be dangerous for him to leave the ship, and honestly, he didn't want to. He loved sailing. More than he loved Joanna.

Chapter 8

It had been a week since they left Carolsport, and Christopher couldn't help the slight guilt he had at leaving Joanna the way he had. He should have listened to Henry, and now he not only felt guilty over leaving Joanna with the promise to write to her, but he also felt irritated that his friend was angry with him over it. Henry had barely said a word to him since they got back on board the ship.

Since Henry wasn't talking to him, he turned his attention toward others who were. Pierre quickly became someone he enjoyed talking to. He had good stories, and some bad ones, but he was interesting either way. Pierre even convinced Christopher to grow a goatee. Saying it would make him look older and more of a proper pirate.

"So I went after the bastard and ran him through," Pierre grinned one night over a bottle of rum.

Christopher found he enjoyed drinking with Pierre but knew his limit of rum, and he stuck to it, no matter how much Pierre goaded him to more. He had secrets to keep and couldn't afford to let them out.

"Did you get back the gold he took?" Christopher asked with a grin.

"I did. Then I spent it on more rum and a nice girl with red hair," Pierre said happily before he took another swig of the bottle. "If we're ever in that little port again I'll introduce you to her. She'll make you forget your troubles," Pierre winked at him and Christopher grew sober.

"He doesn't need help finding girls," Cale interrupted, "He found one in England without even trying. Left her crying on the dock."

Pierre looked at Christopher impressed.

"Ah, so you're one of those. I knew you were pretty, but I'm going to be irritated if I have to compete with you over wenches."

Christopher shook his head, "Don't worry about me, Pierre."

Cale snickered and Christopher glared at him.

Christopher looked towards Henry out of the corner of his eye. His friend wasn't enjoying the conversation. Pierre started a new story and Christopher picked up a bottle of rum and moved to sit next to Henry.

"Are you ever going to forgive me, or are we no longer brothers?" he held out the bottle towards Henry.

Henry gave him a hard stare for a moment, then he sighed and took the bottle.

"I guess there's nothing we can do now. She's already sucked in by your charms," he said sarcastically before taking a swig from the bottle, "You'll always be my brother, no matter how much I want to throw you overboard. I'd just have to fish you out because I like you too much."

Christopher grinned at Henry as Henry took another swig of the rum.

∞∞∞

At the next port, Christopher bought some paper and wrote his first letter to Joanna. He wasn't sure what to tell her at first. He'd never written a letter before. So he eventually decided just to write her a short letter, to begin with.

Joanna,

We are in Florida picking up new cargo. I'm not sure where we will be next, but I think we are headed further south into the Caribbean.

I haven't been able to stop thinking of you since I left. I want you to understand why I couldn't stay with you. The sea calls to me, Joanna. I can't seem to think of myself anywhere but here on the blue sea teaming with life. Just today I saw creatures I was told were dolphins. They jumped out of the water like they were playing. I wish you could have seen them. I know they would have put that beautiful smile on your sweet face.

I was watching a beautiful sunset across the water last night as I stood at the helm. As the last of the sun could be seen on the horizon, the rays shimmered off the water in such a way as I could see violet. It was like looking into your lovely eyes. I miss your laughter and wish I was there to stop the tears that I'm sure will be running down your soft cheeks.

I would wipe them from your cheeks with my finger and then kiss you until you were no longer sad. Know that I'm thinking of you as I watch each sunset. Looking for your violet eyes.

Love,

C.L. James

Christopher found a ship heading back north and sent his letter off, hoping it made it to its destination. Then he went to find Henry and Pierre at a tavern nearby.

They spent a few days in Jamaica trading cargo, and Christopher wrote Joanna they were headed for France next. What he didn't tell her was they had to stop and meet up with Captain Brambell. The man who had turned Maria into a pirate ship. They had to give him what they owed him thus far from their trades. The original crew of the Maria was nervous about meeting up with the pirate ship again. Nothing good could come from the meeting.

They met the other ship about a week out into their crossing to France. The ships pulled up alongside each other, and

Captain Hunter called the crew to stand on deck to receive the great Captain Brambell. They all stood waiting nervously as a plank was put between the ships. Then they watched as the man with red hair and a scraggly red beard walked across the plank and down onto their ship.

He hardly looked at the crew before gesturing to Captain Hunter to take him to the cabin. They went to the captain's cabin and were there for roughly half an hour before the crew's attention was drawn by yelling.

"But I didn't, sir! I swear I didn't!"

The door to the cabin opened and Captain Hunter stumbled out, followed closely by Captain Brambell. Hunter looked downright scared, and it made Christopher happy to see the man graveling at Brambell's feet.

"This deceptive scum didn't do what I asked of him. He didn't make me hardly any money, and then he tried to cheat me out of what he owed me. Who here wants his job?"

No one moved.

"The man who can come up here, and put this worm out of his misery can have his job."

Something came over Christopher, and he suddenly took out his sword and walked up the steps. He walked over to Brambell and Hunter but didn't look at Brambell. Without blinking, he ran his sword through Hunter's heart and pulled it back out.

Hunter slumped to the ground and coughed up blood. But Christopher wasn't done. He replaced his sword in its sheath before he bent over and grabbed Hunter by his vest collar. He dragged him to the edge of the ship and propped him up on the side. Then he pushed the man back and watched as he fell off the side, into the depths below.

Christopher turned and looked at Brambell.

Brambell looked at Christopher with admiration.

"Good. Come inside. I'll show you what I want you to do."

Christopher walked towards the captain and glanced down to see Henry looking at him with shock, right before he went inside.

∞∞∞

Christopher stepped into the office of captain with ease. He enjoyed giving orders instead of taking them, but he also found it to be lonelier. The men wouldn't talk and drink with him like they usually did. Henry stayed away for the first few days. If Henry wasn't at the helm, he was working on something else. Christopher hadn't been able to explain to him yet. Robert had been the one to bring him his things from the lower deck.

So one night he sent for Henry and ordered him to come to the captain's cabin. Robert was talking about the day's sailing when Henry knocked on the door. Christopher could see that Henry was stern in his manner.

"Thank you, Robert," Christopher said dismissively.

Robert left and Christopher looked at Henry from his seat at the desk.

"Henry, I know what you're thinking, but I swear I did it for a good reason."

Henry didn't say anything but just stood staring straight ahead.

"Hunter deserved what he got. What he did to Brack was sick. Surely I can do better, treat the men better. They won't have to be fearful all the time."

Henry looked at him now with a frown, "You don't think what you did was just as bad?"

Christopher stood, "Are you serious? Brack suffered as he died. What I did was merciful in comparison. Who knows what sick death Brambell had planned if no one stepped up," he stood in front of Henry and his voice softened, "Please, I need you by my side. I can't lose your friendship. Please don't turn your back on me now."

Henry seemed to soften his stance a little and stared

thoughtfully at Christopher.

"Alright, I'll not give up on you yet," Henry said as he nodded slightly.

"Thank you," Christopher gestured to the chair in front of the desk, "Sit?"

Christopher moved around to sit behind the desk and Henry sat in front. Christopher set a bottle on the desk.

"Drink with me?" Christopher asked.

Henry hesitated.

"Nothing's changed, Henry. We're friends first. You can talk to me like always. I wouldn't have it any other way."

Henry stared at Christopher a moment more before he picked up the bottle, "The pirates that came on board with Hunter aren't too happy with you. Some think it's unfair how you became captain. The right way to become captain is by voting. Whoever wins the vote gets to be captain. There was no vote, so they are not happy."

"Mutiny?"

Henry shook his head, "I'm not sure they want to cross Brambell. They may be more afraid of him," Henry handed the bottle over to Christopher, "I wouldn't be surprised though if you put yourself in a position where you have to show you can be as ruthless as Hunter."

Christopher looked at Henry with surprise.

"You didn't like me killing Hunter, and now you want me to be like him?"

"I'm not saying I want you to, but don't be surprised if they push back on you. Test your authority. What are you going to do if they do?"

Christopher thought about it while he took a swig of the bottle, "I don't know."

"Well, you better figure it out. I won't be surprised if someone tests you in the next few days."

Christopher nodded, "Alright."

"What do you know about being a captain anyway? That's another thing they aren't happy about. We're still new here.

We don't know half as much as the others. They don't think someone as green as you or me should be captain."

"If they wanted the job, then they should have stepped forward. They didn't. I did. Robert is helping me. He said he was just glad it wasn't him and he's more than willing to help me learn. I figure as long as I act like I know what I'm doing, I'll fool them until I do. Besides, I'm not ignorant. I know more than you give me credit for."

Henry grinned, "Good, I'm glad to hear you're smarter than you look."

Christopher picked up a pencil and threw it at Henry. Henry dodged it with a laugh. He picked it up and set the pencil on the desk before holding out his hand for the bottle. Christopher took another swig before giving it to Henry.

"It's good to see you smile again my friend," Christopher said as Henry took another drink.

Henry sobered a little, "There's not always something to smile about. This is harder than I expected it to be."

Christopher nodded, "I agree."

"We didn't know what it was really like being pirates when we were kids. I always thought it would be freeing to be able to do whatever you like. But there are more rules and less freedom than I expected. And the only way out is to die."

Christopher nodded thoughtfully.

"My offer still stands if you want to take it," Christopher said seriously, "I'll say you're dead should anyone ask."

Henry smiled, "Thanks, but if I go, who will watch out for you?"

Christopher sobered, "You won't like what I have to do next."

Henry frowned slightly, "What do you mean?"

"Captain Brambell wants me to find someone wealthy in France. Someone who wants to travel to the Americas. Offer them a ride, and then hand them over to Brambell so he can ransom them. We'll get half the ransom."

"Will he hurt them when we turn them over?"

"I don't know. I don't think so. I'd think he'd want to protect them so that he gets the money. He didn't say any different."

"He's a pirate, Chris. He can't be trusted."

"I know, but I don't have a choice. This is my test. If I don't pull this off I'll be the next dead captain."

Henry sat thoughtfully for a minute, and then a knock at the door came.

"Enter," Christopher said loudly.

Robert entered, "I think the new helmsman is working out. He's not as bright as you two, but he'll do."

"Good," Christopher handed the bottle to Robert, "I was just telling Henry about our mission."

Robert looked at him with surprise.

"There are no secrets between Henry and me," Christopher explained.

"I was just going to say that we should ensure we find a man to ransom. Who knows what Brambell would do with a woman," Henry spoke up.

Robert shook his head, "No, actually a woman would be better. He'd treat her like a queen. Pirates don't like females aboard because they're superstitious. They are afraid females bring bad luck. He'll want to take care of her so that she gets off safe, and the sooner the better. If we bring him a man, he may just kill him and deliver a dead body, or none at all."

Henry looked at Christopher with surprise.

"You can't think it's alright to take some girl and put her in that kind of danger?"

Christopher shrugged, "We may not have a choice. We'll just have to see who we can find first," Christopher held up a piece of paper, "There's a man who works for Brambell in France. His name is Mr. Mendall. He'll put me onto people who are wealthy and looking for a ship to the Americas. We'll have to see who he's found."

Christopher opened a drawer in the desk and pulled out a box, "Look what I found, Henry."

"A chessboard?" Henry looked surprised.

"How about a game?"

"I don't know, my watch comes early in the morning."

"Just one game."

"Alright."

"I've never learned to play chess," Robert said after he took another drink from the bottle.

"Stick around and we'll teach you," Christopher said with a small smile.

∞∞∞

A couple of days later, Henry's worry came to pass. Boatswain Timmy the Stretch was ordering some men to roll up a sail, and Christopher overheard him.

"I just finished ordering them to unroll the sail, Mr. Stretch," Christopher said sternly. Then he nodded to the sailors and they unrolled it again.

Stretch mumbled something under his breath, and Christopher could tell he was cursing him.

"What was that, Mr. Stretch?" Christopher said louder.

"Nothing, Captain," Stretch growled.

Sailors were starting to listen and turn their attention toward the two of them.

"That's not what it sounded like," Christopher said, goading the man.

"I said you were a bastard who doesn't know nothing about sailing," Stretch spat out.

"Are you questioning my abilities, Mr. Stretch?"

"Yes," Stretch said defiantly, "You're a low-down scum who should be at the bottom of the ocean deep, instead of Captain Hunter! You don't know nothing, boy." Stretch looked up at the sailors who had stopped unrolling the sail to listen, "Roll that up tight. Don't listen to this chump."

"Mr. Stretch, are you declaring mutiny?" Christopher looked at the man darkly.

Stretch glared at Christopher and yelled, "Yes, I think we should all vote for a new captain. Someone who knows what they're do'n. If we don't we'll all end up dead, because this boy will disappoint Brambell and he'll kill us all. Let someone like me be captain. I won't disappoint him!"

No one moved, and everyone stayed silent as they stared at Christopher and Stretch.

"Cob," Christopher called to Robert, "Remove his shirt, and tie Mr. Stretch facing the mast."

"Yes, sir," Robert said as he waved to Henry and Pierre to join him.

Between the three of them, they were able to get Stretch tied to the mast with his bare back facing out. While they did this, Christopher ran back to his cabin and came back with a long black whip.

He stood before the crew and looked around to make sure they were listening.

"I am not Hunter. I don't shove men in barrels and toss them overboard to drown. But I can't have discipline lacking on my ship, and you *will* follow my orders. I know what I must do to please Brambell and I will do it. I will not have my men questioning my judgment or talking of mutiny. If you feel like doing so, then you can join your friend Mr. Stretch at the mast today," He looked around again, "Anyone want to join him?"

No one moved or said a word.

Christopher raised his arm and brought the whip down with a snap. A pain-filled cry came from Stretch. Another flick of the whip and another cry from Stretch. It was all Christopher could do to keep his face emotionless and keep going. What he wanted to do was to stop and help Stretch, but that wasn't an option for him. He was the captain now, and it was his responsibility to keep his men in line.

True, he could have had Robert do the actual whipping, but at this moment he had to show his strength to the crew. To show he was strong enough, and tough enough, to do the job he had volunteered for. If they didn't follow him then he would lose his position quickly and maybe even die.

He reached thirty and wanted to vomit his dinner rations, just at the sight of Stretch's back. The man moaned now instead of crying out. He was slumped against the mast. Christopher was disgusted by the sight, and even more, disgusted knowing he was the cause of such a sight.

He finally made it to forty and stopped. He nodded to Robert and moved away towards the stairs. When he looked back, he saw Henry and Cale taking Stretch off the mast carefully. Knowing he had done that to someone, put them in that kind of pain, made him sick with himself.

"It had to be done," he told himself as he turned and walked into his cabin.

Chapter 9

They sailed through a small storm on their way, but they made it safely to Le Havre, France. Christopher went to find Mr. Mendall and found the slim man in a shipping office.

"I deal with many wealthy people, sir. I'm very good at my job." He paused with a cold stare that seemed to penetrate Christopher's heart. "Both of my jobs. I've never been connected to the ransoms that Brambell makes. I'm excellent at my work, and if you want to stay alive you'll do exactly what I say."

"Yes, sir. Just give me a name," Christopher said coldly in return.

"It's not that simple," Mr. Mendall raised his chin as he looked Christopher over judgingly. "There's a woman by the name of Mademoiselle Celeste Delaire. Her father is a very wealthy man, and he's sent for his daughter to live with him and his wife in Jamaica. They wish a safe passage for their beautiful, and troublesome, daughter."

"What do you mean troublesome?" Christopher raised a brow.

"She's got a reputation for being…unscrupulous…with her lovers." Mr. Mendall seemed to be coldly amused now. "She's refused every ship I've offered her. Your job should be easy enough. You must convince her to use your ship for passage. Any way possible."

"What do you mean 'any way possible'?" Though Christopher had a feeling he knew what the man was about to say.

"Seduce her into trusting you enough to take passage aboard your ship."

Christopher stood thoughtfully for a moment before nodding shortly, “Alright. How do I meet her?”

“Tonight, there is a party I’ve been invited to, and I believe she’ll be there. I’ll introduce you to her, and you can take over convincing the lovely Mademoiselle Delaire,” Mr. Mendall went back to his ledgers on his desk, “Be here at 6:00 tonight. I suggest you go find a shop to buy a new suit for the occasion. You’ll want to look as high class as you can for a captain.”

∞∞∞

Christopher went back to the ship to acquire the money he needed and Henry and Robert found him in his cabin.

“The cargo is being unloaded, sir,” Robert said, “Did Mr. Mendall give you a mark?”

Christopher nodded, “Yes, and I will be gone for a while to get what I need to meet her. Keep the men working on the cargo. As soon as it's done, Mr. Mendall will have his man lead you to the new cargo to be loaded. Then restock the ship's supplies. Once that is all done, you can give the men shore leave, but they must be back on the ship each night so I don’t have to find them all when it's time to leave. I don’t know how long we’ll be here.”

“Yes, sir.”

“I’ll also be gone late tonight. Make sure to keep everyone accounted for,” he flicked a coin to Henry who caught it seriously, “Get me some more rum while you're out.”

“Pierre told me on Brambell’s ship they add rum to the water so they don’t have to taste the stale water when it gets hot and old on the crossing. Don’t suppose you’d want to do that?” Henry asked.

“And have constantly drunk pirates on board my ship? I don’t think so. Don’t do that,” Christopher said sternly.

“Yes, sir,” Henry said as Christopher walked towards the door.

Christopher turned to Henry with amusement.

"Why don't you come with me? I have to buy a fancy suit for tonight. You may as well come to make fun of me."

Henry grinned, "I'd be happy too."

Christopher and Henry found a shop to buy a suit of clothes from, for Christopher's evening among the wealthy. Henry did his best to make fun of his friend as he tried things on, but when they found the right clothes, he realized he hoped Joanna never saw Christopher in them.

"You'll have no trouble convincing the lady to use our ship for her travels," Henry said grimly.

"I hope she'll be easy to convince. I don't relish the idea of being around a bunch of pompous wealthy people. I don't really know what to do tonight. Do I just use the manners your mother always taught us? Or is there more than that?"

Henry looked at his friend standing in his black suit, which complimented his black hair and black goatee. He answered wryly, "They won't care about your manners. Especially not the ladies," Henry shook his head, "Women throw themselves at you wherever you go. Every time we leave the ship, some woman flirts with you."

Christopher grinned, "You sound jealous. Maybe we should get you a suit and you can come with me. I'm sure we could find you a lovely lady tonight."

Henry laughed, "I don't want to be dressed up any more than you do. I'm not the one being forced into it."

Christopher shook his head in mock disgust, "Some friend you are, leaving me to the wolves."

"You'll be fine, Chris. Now let's get out of here and find somewhere to eat. I'm tired of rations, and there have to be privileges to being the captain's best friend. I saw a tavern on the way here. Let's get dinner there."

"All right."

When they had the package with Christopher's new clothes and boots, they went to have dinner at the tavern before going back to the ship to help with the cargo.

That evening, Christopher dressed for the party slowly. Trying to remember how everything went on correctly. The only thing he truly liked wearing were the boots. They fit perfectly and he decided he'd wear them daily in the future.

When he finished, he walked quickly to Mr. Mendall's office where he found the man was waiting with a coach for him. They traveled further into the city. The further they got from the docks, the better their surroundings became. Soon large homes started spreading further apart as they started leaving the city and moving into the countryside. They turned down a lane and pulled up in front of a large mansion.

Christopher had never seen anything like it before. He counted ten windows along the front of the house, and that was just the first floor. They walked into a grand hallway that was lined with a mixture of stone and walnut wood panels. After greeting their hosts, they were ushered into a large ballroom filled with people. Beautiful women in exquisite dresses mingled together or with male escorts.

"Remember you are a ship captain, sir," Mr. Mendall said quietly.

Christopher looked at him confused, "Yes?"

"You look nervous. Just remember to feed their imaginations about life on a ship, but tell them very little truth about yourself. You want them to be enamored with who you are, but know nothing about you."

Christopher nodded and straightened with more confidence.

Mr. Mendall led him through the crowd until they reached a group of ladies who were sitting together on settees and chairs. Christopher's attention went straight to a beautiful woman with golden tresses and blue eyes that were almost teal. Her perfect red lips moved upward into a smile when she locked eyes with him. He felt his heart beat a little faster.

Mr. Mendall stepped up to the intriguing woman, took her hand, and kissed it.

"Mademoiselle Delaire, I'd like to introduce you to

Captain James. His ship may be one you consider for your travels."

They hadn't taken their eyes off each other since he walked up, and Christopher couldn't see anyone else in the room. He slowly stepped forward and took her hand the way Mendall had. Leaning down, without taking his eyes from hers, he kissed her hand softly.

"It is my undying pleasure to meet you, mademoiselle," he said softly.

Suddenly music started from somewhere, but their eyes remained on one another.

Celeste stared at the handsome captain and her heart skipped. She had never seen a more handsome man and wanted nothing more than to be closer to him.

"I think you should ask me to dance, Captain," she said with an enchanting voice.

He smiled, "I would, but I'm afraid I have a secret."

She smiled in return and leaned forward, whispering, "What is it?"

He leaned over and his breath tickled her ear as he whispered, "I don't know how to dance."

She turned her face to his with a seductive smile, "Then I shall have to teach you."

Celeste held out her hand to him and he straightened as he took it. She rose and they made their way to the dance floor. She took one of his hands in hers and moved the other one to hold her around the waist. Then she guided him around the room until he seemed to figure it out.

Christopher couldn't stop staring at her. He found her beautiful and mysterious. She smiled at him coyly.

"You are staring, Captain."

"Am I?" He said as though he didn't care, "I think you know why."

"Are you saying I'm vain, Captain?" she said with amusement.

"I'm saying there's not a man in this room who doesn't

know how beautiful you are. And you know it. I'm just the lucky one who got to have you for the first dance."

"You're rather young to be a captain," she said with interest.

"As I said, I'm lucky," he said softly.

They danced for a while without talking, focusing on the moment. When the song ended, his arm went around her tighter and he pulled her close, but to his annoyance, they were suddenly interrupted by someone tapping on his shoulder.

"I would like the next dance with the mademoiselle," a man said.

Christopher relinquished his hold on her and kissed her hand before bowing a little and walking away without looking back. Finding Mr. Mendall in the crowd, he joined him to continue watching Mademoiselle Delaire as she danced.

"She can't keep her eyes off of you," Mr. Mendall observed as they watched. "You've succeeded in getting her attention. Now you must convince her to go on your ship."

"One thing at a time," Christopher said as he watched her dance gracefully across the room.

He continued to watch her as she danced with two other men before he saw her slip off the dance floor and look at him pointedly before she walked to a door that led outside. He made his way through the crowd around the dance floor until he reached the door, and stepped out to find her standing on a balcony overlooking the gardens.

"I was wondering how long it would take you to follow me," She purred as she turned around.

Christopher walked over to her, resting his hands on the balcony railing. One hand on either side of her, trapping her.

"Was there any doubt I'd come?"

"I can never tell for sure if a man has the intelligence to follow when I wish him to. Some of them are pretty but stupid."

"Well, I'm here," he smirked, "Now what do you want?"

"To tell you my name."

"I already know your name, Celeste."

"Yes, but only my friends and lovers call me Cece."

She put her hands on either side of his face and ran her fingers along his jaw. Her touch made his heart race even faster.

"I prefer Celeste," he said as he moved closer, pressing her against the balcony railing and moving his arms around her back. "Is that all that I am? Your conquest?"

"No, darling," she said breathlessly, before pulling his head down and pressing her lips onto his.

They kissed passionately until Christopher could no longer think about anything except her lips. His brain was in a fog and his hand moved to her face where he held her jaw and neck. Kissing her ardently. When he felt he couldn't breathe, he pulled back to stop, but she pulled his head down again. He had never been kissed so passionately and he wanted nothing more than to keep doing so forever.

Suddenly the door opened and she pushed him away as one of her friends came rushing out.

"Cece, you must come, it's your favorite dance, and George is going to dance with you."

Celeste looked at Christopher, and he just stared at her while he rubbed his thumb across his chin and mouth. Then she smiled coyly at him.

"Alright," and with that she left him standing there, looking after her.

He took several deep breaths, trying to regain control and clear the fog in his brain. It only partly helped. Then he walked back inside and made his way around the ballroom until he found Mr. Mendall.

"Things going well, I presume?"

"I'd like to think so, but she's unpredictable. Even if I could convince her tonight, it doesn't mean she would agree again tomorrow. I have a feeling she's playing with me."

"You're intelligent to see it. Now use it to get her on your ship."

"I will. It just may take time."

"You don't have a lot of time. If you can't get her to sail

with you in a week's time, I'll have to try the next ship Brambell sends me. He won't be happy with you. I don't have anyone else right now."

"Fine, I'll do my best to work fast. Now get off my back and let me do my job."

Mr. Mendell smirked knowingly.

"I don't suppose there's anything to drink?" Christopher looked around.

"You'll find some wine in the next room."

Christopher looked at Celeste once more, and she at him before he walked through the crowd and out the door into the hall. He followed some people into a smaller room where servants served a variety of foods and drinks. Christopher found a servant with crystal goblets with a dark liquid in them. He took one and took a sip. It was sweeter and more subtle than the rum and ale he was used to drinking.

"Did you bore of watching me so soon?" Celeste's sweet voice came from behind him.

He turned slowly with a smirk.

"You don't think I'd want to watch you in the arms of another man now? It's rather insulting. I'd like to think a woman would be smarter than to let a good man go just to flirt with another man under his nose. Besides, I needed a drink after..."

She put her finger to his lips to stop him from saying "kissing" and she looked around to see who might be listening.

"Maybe you're the one who is bored," he said, still smirking. Then he took another drink of the wine and turned slightly away from her.

"Don't say that, Captain. I could never become bored of a handsome man like you."

"Maybe you're just bored in general, Celeste," he said with a slight shrug, "Maybe you should try some adventure."

Celeste moved in front of him and fingered his collar as she looked up at him with a smile.

"What kind of adventure do you mean, Captain?"

"The kind of adventure you only get if you sail with me to

the Americas."

"Mmm," she turned and picked up a small round pastry from a tray. Then she turned back and held it up to him, "Maybe you are the one who is bored, my captain."

He stared at her for a moment before letting her feed him the pastry. It was filled with something sweet and it was delicious but he didn't let it linger in his thoughts.

"Do you like it, Captain?" she asked sweetly with a tempting smile and a hand on his arm.

He stepped closer to her and reached to touch her lips with his thumb.

"Delicious."

She looked mesmerized and then blinked and her smile came back to coy. She turned and reached for a different food and giggled when he rolled his eyes at her wanting to feed him.

"I can feed myself. I've been doing it my whole life," he said with slight irritation.

She moved close to him again and whispered, "Indulge me, Captain."

He stared into her eyes deeply for a moment before he leaned forward and took the bite she held out to him, but he didn't take his eyes from hers. When she took another pastry and held it out to him, he grabbed her wrist and turned her hand back towards her. She took the bite while looking at him with surprise. He released her and finished his drink.

He walked away from her and gave his glass to a servant as he took a new one. He drank it quickly and gave it back to the servant. Then he took her arm, pulling her towards the door.

"I think you owe me another dance."

He took her back out to the dance floor and pulled her into his arms. They danced several songs before she pretended to beg him to stop because she was tired.

"I think we should talk about your ship some more tomorrow evening over supper," she said quietly, "Mr. Mendall can tell you where I live. He's been working for my family for a while now. Be there at 8:00. Don't be late, my love."

"I won't," He raised her hand to his lips and his kiss lingered, "Good night."

Then he released her and she walked away. He watched her leave before he went to find Mr. Mendall.

∞∞∞

Christopher stepped aboard his ship and Henry saw him go to his cabin and followed him.

"How did it go?" Henry asked as Christopher took off the jacket and flung it to his bed. Then he took out a bottle from his desk and took a long drink. "Well?" Henry asked impatiently.

Christopher plunked down into his chair, "She's exquisite. And trouble. And I have almost no self-control around her." He broodingly took another drink, "Now get out, because I don't want to talk about her. I just want to drink. Alone."

Henry stared at Christopher for a moment. All he could think of was Joanna, and how his friend was going to break her heart. He stood and went to the door. He took one more look at his brooding friend before slamming the door behind him.

Chapter 10

Celeste donned her prettiest dress and her maid created a cascade of curly golden hair down her back. She wanted to look as tempting as she could for the captain's arrival.

She had found him intriguing and wanted nothing more than to have him kiss her again. If she had her way, he'd stay with her tonight, and she'd happily wake up in his arms the next morning.

She smiled at herself in the mirror before leaving her room and joining her friend in the sitting room to wait for him.

∞∞∞

Christopher was right on time when he arrived at Celeste's home. A man in a suit and white gloves let him in and escorted him to a door where the man knocked before stepping in to announce Christopher.

"Captain James is here, Mademoiselles."

"Send him in," said a voice as the man moved aside so Christopher could enter.

He ignored the fine things everywhere and focused on the two ladies sitting in the room. Celeste sat beautifully in a pink dress on the settee. Christopher glanced at the other lady who was sitting with her dark brown hair piled on her head and green eyes shining with amusement.

Christopher bowed slightly to both ladies, and he stared at Celeste.

"Thank you for having me," he said to her.

"It is to me you should be thanking." The other woman interrupted, "This is my home you have entered."

He looked at her more carefully and bowed again to her, "I'm sorry, mademoiselle. I was led to believe this was Mademoiselle Delaire's home. Please, forgive me."

The woman rose and came to him. Her green dress swayed as she walked. She put a delicate hand on his arm and her eyes fluttered as she looked up at him. A glance at Celeste told him she was amused and this irritated him, so he turned to the woman, took her hand, and pressed his lips to her palm.

"May I have the honor of knowing to whom I am only now meeting in her beautiful home?" he said, flirting with the woman openly.

"I'm Lilou, and it's a pleasure to finally meet you, Captain."

"Please, call me James," he let his gaze linger on her eyes.

"Only if you call me Lilou," she said smiling up at him.

"Lilou!" Celeste's voice came sharply.

Lilou stepped back from him with an amused smile. Christopher turned to look at Celeste innocently as she came to him with a stern look.

"I didn't invite you here to be with Lilou," she said annoyed.

He smirked as he took her hand in his, "If I didn't know any better, I'd say you're jealous. Jealousy doesn't look good on a woman," he raised her hand and kissed her palm softly.

"I'll forgive you just this once for saying that something doesn't look good on me," she said softly.

"Supper is ready, mademoiselle," a servant said from behind him.

"Thank you," Lilou responded. "If you are both done greeting each other, we should have supper." Her voice betrayed her amusement.

Christopher put Celeste's hand in the crook of his arm and they followed Lilou out of the room to a dining room where he helped the ladies sit and then sat across the table from Celeste.

"Where all have you sailed to, James?" Lilou asked him as they started eating.

"Well, mostly we go wherever our cargo needs to go. I've been to England, America, Jamaica, France."

"And where are you from?" Lilou asked gracefully.

"America."

"What is your favorite place that you've traveled to?" Lilou asked before taking a bite.

He looked at Celeste, "Jamaica. Beautiful country. The people are some of the finest I've ever met."

"I've heard it's hot and uncivilized," Celeste said with a wrinkle of disgust on her nose.

"It is hot, but its beauty makes up for it. As for uncivilized I've heard the plantation owners have plenty of parties of their own. You would be like a shining jewel among them all, I'm sure." He looked at her innocently, "That is where your family is now, correct?"

She looked at him annoyed, "You know it is."

"Don't you wish to join them in paradise?"

"Not particularly," she rolled her eyes, "Though my father is demanding I go."

"Well, I guess it's just your luck we are headed there," he said nonchalantly.

"You're going to Jamaica now?" she asked curiously.

"Mmhmm," he took another bite of his meal.

"When do you have to leave?"

"Well, I'd like to leave as soon as we can get our cargo loaded," he said thoughtfully, "But if you wish to join us, then I could be persuaded to wait for you."

She stared at him a moment and then smiled coyly.

"I think you should abandon your ship and stay with me."

He smirked, "And why would I give up my ship to stay with a woman?"

Celeste pouted and stood. Then she huffed out of the room. He looked at Lilou with surprise, but she just smiled at him with amusement. He took that to mean he was supposed to follow the dramatic Celeste, so he rose and walked out of the room to find her. He found her in the sitting room on the settee, looking her best at being mad at him. He could have babied her and gently persuaded her, but he chose a different approach.

Christopher went to sit next to her and she turned away. He grabbed her shoulders roughly turning her back to him, and caught her in his arms. Then he grabbed her head with one hand and kissed her furiously.

Finally, she broke free to gasp for air, and she looked at him with a little fear, and wonder.

"Captain?" she whispered.

Christopher looked at her ardently. "James," he corrected.

He kissed her again, but more gently, and she melted into his embrace. She was warm and felt good in his arms. He deepened the kiss and her hands wrapped around his neck. He pushed her and she willingly laid back on the settee. He moved to kiss her neck, and down her neckline, before moving back to her lips.

Celeste pushed him back enough that he stopped kissing her and looked at her. She reached to unbutton his shirt and he suddenly knew what she wanted and knew how he was going to entice her to board his ship. He stopped her by grabbing her wrist. She looked at him confused.

"What's wrong?" she asked.

"I'm leaving. I can't stay with you. I can't leave my ship. It's all I've ever wanted."

"But you love me," she pouted beautifully.

"You intrigue me." He leaned down to kiss her again fervently. Then he stopped suddenly. "Come with me. Let me take you to Jamaica."

She frowned at him.

"But you will leave me when we get to Jamaica."

"Yes," he shrugged, "but we'll have the whole month together on the way there." He kissed her again, "Come with me," he said as his lips moved to her neck.

"I will come but I want you to stay with me until it's time

to go," she tried the button at the top of his shirt again but he grabbed her wrist and pulled it away.

"No," he said firmly as he trapped Celeste's wrist against the settee before returning his lips to hers.

When Christopher released her from his kiss she looked at him through dazed eyes.

"I find I can't say no to you," she said softly. She ran her thumb across his mouth and he kissed it, "Stay with me, just tonight."

"I cannot. I have to see my men. We leave in two days."

He stood up and pulled her up beside him. Then leaned down to kiss her forehead softly.

"I'll be back tomorrow evening for your trunks. Have them ready," he said as he released her.

"You're leaving?" Celeste said surprised as he moved a step back.

"I have work to do. I'll be back tomorrow."

He took her hand and kissed her palm. Then let it go as he walked away and out the door.

Celeste watched him in awe. Had she just said yes to leaving with him? She hated the idea of Jamaica and wanted to stay in her beloved France. But she couldn't help but want nothing more than to be stuck aboard a ship with such a man for a month!

∞∞∞

Christopher walked down the street after returning Mr. Mendall's carriage and found the tavern the men had been going to. He walked in and saw Henry, Cale, and Robert sitting together. He started towards them but when he looked at Henry, his thoughts went to Joanna and he stopped. Guilt and anger flooded him. The men looked at him with questioning frowns, but he turned on his heel and walked back out of the tavern. He quickly made his way back to the ship and to his cabin, where he proceeded to change his clothes and then drink a bottle of rum before passing out on his bed.

∞∞∞

"Let me help you." Christopher took hold of Celeste's waist and lifted her off the side of the ship. She stood in front of him with a beautiful smile and he stared at her with a desire to kiss her perfect lips. Robert cleared his throat, and he looked up at him irritably.

"Do you want us to set sail now, sir?"

"Of course," Christopher nearly growled at Robert.

Robert nodded slightly and turned to give orders to the men.

"Come." Christopher took Celeste's hand and tucked it in the crook of his arm. "I'll show you to my cabin."

She smiled up at him and the desire he hadn't been able to quench with a bottle of rum came flooding back. He suddenly glanced up and saw Henry staring at him from the helm.

Christopher frowned with irritation and looked away. He had a job to do, and he would deliver. He deserved to be admired for getting their mark on board, not guilt-laden because of someone he would likely never see again. Celeste was here with him now. She was beautiful and already knew they had no future together. Yet she still wanted him. As he took her hand to lead her up the stairs her smile shined up at him and he let himself relax.

"I had both your trunks put in here with you," he said as he opened the door to his cabin. "You won't be bothered here. My men have orders to not come unless called. I will bring you your meals myself. Unfortunately, it'll just be rationing. I'm sorry we can't give you something better, but we can't accommodate more on such a long journey." He leaned down to gently brush his lips on her forehead. “Thank you for letting me sail you across the sea, mademoiselle.”

Celeste smiled at him sweetly, “You’re very welcome, captain. May we watch as they set sail?”

“Of course.” He took her hand again and led her back outside to take in the activities as the crew put the ship into motion and moved slowly out of the harbor.

While Celeste watched the men work with great interest, he took her in. Her face lit up as she with each movement and change the men made to make the huge sails unfurl. The sun glimmered off her jeweled hairpin with every movement of her head, and her eyes were intent with interest. When she caught him staring at her, she gave a melodious little laugh.

“What?” she asked as she stepped closer to him.

“I just like watching you. You’re so interested.”

“It's interesting to see how the ship moves as the men work.” her delicate eyebrows frowned slightly as she looked back at the men. “But how does it turn?”

“That's what the helm does. It steers the ship,” he pointed to the wheel that Henry stood steering.

“May I see?”

She asked so sweetly he couldn’t say no, so he led her up to the top deck and over to Henry at the helm.

“Mademoiselle Delaire, this is my most trusted helmsman, Liam. He can explain what the helm does.” As he introduced them he stared at Henry in curiosity. He wasn’t sure what Henry would do. But he should have given Henry more credit.

Henry smiled at her kindly, “Hello, miss. You want to learn about the helm?”

Celeste nodded.

“This big wheel is attached to a rudder under the ship. When I turn the helm it turns the rudder, and that turns the ship where we want it to go.” Henry explained everything happily and Christopher relaxed.

Celeste turned to look at Christopher and put her hands

on his chest.

"May I try?" she asked very sweetly again and he couldn't resist.

Christopher took her hands and moved to take Henry's place at the helm. He placed her hands on the wheel and stood behind her closely while keeping his hands on hers. She laughed joyfully and he couldn't help but smile and kiss the back of her head.

Another ship was coming towards them, so Christopher took her hands off the helm and steered his ship away from the other. He nodded at Henry to take the helm again, and Henry moved to do so. Christopher took Celeste's hand and stepped away. She tugged him towards the back of the ship where they could see Le Havre disappearing.

Celeste put her hands on the railing and watched with sadness. Christopher leaned against the railing, watching Celeste.

"Will you miss it?" he asked softly.

"It's why I didn't want to leave. I love my life in France. I had no wish to go." Then she looked at him and smiled coyly as she stepped towards him, "I couldn't help but want you too much to stay though." Her fingers traced his jawline and ended at his lips. "You intrigue me, Captain."

She put her hands on his chest and drew close. He put an arm around her waist and pulled her tightly. Then he put his other hand on the side of her face.

"James," he said softly.

"James," she smiled coyly again, "Aren't you going to kiss me?"

He looked around and saw only Robert and Henry on the deck, and they were looking at charts. He turned back to her and leaned down to kiss her.

He meant to give her just a short kiss, but her hands caught his head and she kissed him more. He responded in kind and when they stopped, his head felt like it was in a fog again. From the corner of his eye, he saw Robert wave to him. He nodded slightly and then looked at Celeste.

"I'll be right back." He released her to walk to Robert and Henry. "What is it?" he asked crossly.

"We just wanted to make sure about our destination. Are we to meet up with Brambell still?" Robert asked.

Christopher frowned, "What do you mean still?"

Henry crossed his arms in front of his chest. "You looked pretty cozy with the mark. Are you sure you want to hand her over to that pirate?"

Christopher glared at both men.

"I didn't get her on board just to keep her from Brambell. If we don't give her to him, he'll kill us all for running his ransom away from him," Christopher said darkly. "You want to tell him we took his prize to Jamaica for him?"

Both men shook their heads slowly.

"Then head us towards the meeting coordinates and get us there fast. The sooner she's there the sooner she'll get home."

"Yes, sir," Robert nodded and looked at the map.

"Captain." Henry looked at him seriously, "You know she'll be hurt about what you're going to do with her? She'll hate you."

"You don't think I've thought of that?" Christopher glared at him. "There's nothing I can do about it." Then his face changed from irritated to worried. "I'm more concerned about her telling people about our ship being a pirate ship. We may not be able to return as a regular merchant ship after this. I've got to find a way to make it seem like we don't have a choice but to hand her over to him." He looked back at Celeste thoughtfully.

"Maybe we could convince Brambell to play along and pretend to take her from us forcefully," Robert spoke up.

"Do you think he'd really do that?" Christopher frowned.

"Maybe if it means he can keep using us for runs like this. If we can stay a merchant ship, then no one will suspect us to be a ransom ship. If we could do this again for him, then he might play along."

"I'll think about it," Christopher nodded, "thank you."

"She won't hate you that way," Henry said quietly.

Christopher looked at Henry seriously.

"I have every intention of making sure she hates me before she leaves."

Henry and Robert both frowned at him in worry.

"What are you going to do?" Henry asked.

Christopher walked away toward Celeste.

Chapter 11

“Why do you leave the door open when you work in here, my love?” Celeste asked as she ran her hands down Christopher's chest from behind him, as he sat at his desk. His heart started to pound at her touch. Turning, he pulled her around the chair and onto his lap. It had been a week since they left France, and he enjoyed having her in his cabin while he worked.

“I'm just trying to save your reputation. We wouldn't want your parents worrying about you when they see us.”

She laughed and he looked at her wryly.

“What?” he asked.

“You're so sweet, but my reputation hasn't been a factor in my happiness since I was young.” She leaned over to kiss him until he dropped the pencil in his hand.

“Sir, we have those...” Robert interrupted and stopped short as they looked at him. “Sorry, sir.”

“It's alright, Cob. Come in,” Christopher said, trying to regain control of himself.

“No, it's not,” Celeste pouted, “I want you to myself.” She stood and walked around the desk and towards the door. “Go away, Cob,” she ordered.

Robert looked unsure of what to do. Then Henry walked up with a tray of tea and stopped short at Celeste's words. Unsure of what was going on, Henry looked between Robert and Christopher.

Celeste reached for the door.

“Go away, both of you. The captain will be busy for a while. Don't come back unless he calls you,” she commanded sternly. Then she slammed the door in their faces and barred it.

"Celeste." Christopher's voice came sternly through the door.

Henry and Robert looked at each other.

Henry glanced at Robert, perplexed.

Robert looked at Henry carefully, "I think Celeste has other plans for the good captain this evening. I wouldn't expect to see him for a while."

Irritated, Henry walked off to find an unsuspecting sparring partner to take out his frustration.

∞∞∞

Christopher lay staring up at the ceiling with Celeste asleep next to him. Her soft face breathed in contented slumber. But he stared at the ceiling, trying to figure out what had just happened. He felt like someone had stabbed a knife in his heart.

Joanna's beautiful face appeared in his mind and grief struck him. He moved quietly out of bed and dressed quickly. He left the cabin and went up to the top deck where he found Robert at the helm.

Robert didn't say anything. Christopher stopped and looked at the sun setting on the horizon. Just a peek of it shined, sending violet rays across the waters. Emotion built up and stuck in his throat.

"I made a huge mistake, Robert. Now the woman I love will never have me," he said quietly.

Robert nodded slightly, "It happens to the best of us, captain. Do you want my advice?"

"Yes, please."

"Move on, and don't tell your love what happened. It'll just hurt her."

"I don't think I could love her without her knowing the truth. I don't deserve her."

"None of us deserves the love of a good woman. Not

in our line of work. They all deserve better." Robert looked at Christopher seriously, "But my wife still insists she'll love me and no one else."

Christopher looked at Robert with surprise.

"I didn't know you were married."

Robert nodded, "I slipped up once in a moment of weakness. I tried to tell her what happened and she told me she didn't want to know what I did. I don't deserve that good woman, and I know it. I've done nothing but treat her like a queen since. I send her my love with every port I come to. I send her gifts and my earnings. Don't let this one indiscretion keep you from loving her the way she deserves."

Christopher watched the last of the rays disappear and felt his heart harden against the guilt.

"Thank you, Robert."

"You're welcome, sir."

∞∞∞

Christopher stayed away from Celeste after that. When she tried to leave the cabin and find him, he pretended to be too busy to talk to her and sent her back. When he needed something from his cabin he sent Robert to get it. Then one day he made a decision and forged a deceptive letter. He had Robert place it on his desk where it could be easily spotted.

Robert knocked and then opened the door when he heard her answer.

"Sorry to bother you, miss. I just need to put this on the captain's desk for him. Some of us like to write letters to send out when we dock in port. Would you like to have paper and ink to write one to someone in France?"

"No," she said sadly. "Is the captain ever going to come to talk to me? It's been a week since I've seen him. Please tell him to come to me. I need to speak to him."

"I'll tell him, miss," Robert nodded and left, closing the door behind him.

Celeste looked at the desk where Robert had laid the paper. Bored, she walked over to the desk and looked at it.

My dearest Maggie,

This is my last letter. I can no longer ask you to love me from afar. I'm afraid I've been unfaithful and you deserve better. I hope in time you will forgive me, but I don't expect it. I will love you with all my heart, forever. Goodbye, my love.

Yours always,

James

Tears dropped onto the page as she read the letter. Then anger at his betrayal flared up and she went quickly to the door and flung it open. She stomped up the steps to find Christopher talking to Robert and she looked at him with hatred.

Christopher saw her and instantly knew it had worked. She held the letter crumpled in her hand.

"You rogue!" she yelled at him "How dare you seduce me into thinking you loved me when you clearly didn't!" she waved the letter at him.

He went to her and grabbed her wrist, dragging her to the back of the ship.

"I'm sorry, I needed to make my men some better money than what little cargo we could get. Mr. Mendall said your father would pay a lot to make sure you were safely brought to Jamaica. It's money my men could use to send to their families." He said as he pretended to try to convince her. Then he became angry too. "You used me as well."

She looked at him sharply, "I only asked for what I knew you wanted."

"I tried to stop you."

"You didn't try hard enough."

He looked at her sternly and then softened his grip on her wrist.

"I'm sorry. What has happened has ruined what I had. You're right. It's my own fault. I fell for you and I couldn't keep control. I'm sorry I hurt you."

"I will not let my father pay you all he would. Then I will make him insist we marry." She looked at him with a dark and conniving smile. "I will make you mine and then I will keep you from stepping foot on this ship again."

He tightened his hold on her wrist again in anger.

"You're spoiled. You think you can have whatever you want. Well, you can't. I won't marry you and I won't give up my ship."

"You will do it, or I'll tell my father your crew are all pirates and they will all hang."

He looked at her with surprise, "You wouldn't."

"I will."

"You do that and I'll make your life so unpleasant you'll wish you'd never met me," he growled.

"I don't care. I'll be miserable in Jamaica. I may as well have a pretty face to sleep with in that dreadful place," she said sadistically.

"I've had enough of your conniving," he dragged her back down to the cabin and nearly threw her in by her wrist. "You're to stay in here and don't come out again until we reach port." Then he slammed the door shut.

He stood still for a moment, just looking at the door with his hands on his waist. Then he heard her crying and his heart wrenched with guilt. Now he had hurt her. Which was the point. But it still felt terrible. He turned slowly and went back up to the top deck.

"That didn't go well," Henry said sarcastically.

Christopher glared at him.

"Well, you were right. She's good and mad at you now." Henry continued with a smirk.

Christopher looked at Robert and nodded for him to walk away. Robert nodded and walked to the back of the deck. Christopher stepped closer to Henry and looked at him seriously.

"I'm sorry, Henry."

Henry just shook his head in irritation.

"I'm going to write Joanna and tell her I won't be sending any more letters. I'll tell her what I've done and it'll enrage her enough that she'll move on."

Henry didn't reply and Christopher started to turn away.

"Did you ever actually care about Joanna?"

"I didn't realize how much I loved her until I knew she'd never have me again," he paused thoughtfully, "I'd leave the ship for her."

Henry looked at him with surprise, "You would?"

"Yes," Christopher looked at his feet, "But it doesn't matter now."

Then he turned away from Henry and walked down the steps.

∞∞∞

When they were but a week from Florida they spotted Brambell's ship.

Christopher went to his cabin and opened the door, startling Celeste.

"Pirates are coming for us. Stay in here and be quiet. I don't want them to know you're here," he said quickly.

"Pirates?" she looked at him in fear. "What will they do?"

"I don't know. Just stay here and keep quiet."

She nodded as she sat down on the bed nervously.

Then he closed the door and went down to the upper deck to wait for Brambell. When the pirate captain came on board he went straight to Christopher.

"Did you do what I told you to, boy?"

"Yes, sir. We have a woman whose father will pay handsomely for her safe return to Jamaica."

"Good. Where is she?"

"She's in my cabin. But sir, I had an idea," Christopher said nervously. If the man didn't like something Christopher said or did, he might be at the bottom of the ocean soon.

"What?"

"If we just hand her over to you she'll tell everyone she knows that the Maria is a pirate ship. We won't be able to operate like a merchant. That wouldn't be a problem if it didn't hinder us from acquiring you another ransom. If we stay a merchant ship, then we can continue getting you ransoms from Europe."

"What did you have in mind?" Brambell asked, intrigued.

"Put all my men at sword point and beat me in front of her. She'll believe we tried to save her, and then we'll be free to go for another mark after we deliver our cargo."

Brambell stared at him for a moment and then grinned evilly. "It seems you've given this great thought. Alright, I'll play along with your theatrics."

Brambell looked at his first mate, "Send more men over and put these men on their knees."

"Yes, sir," the man went to do as ordered. As the men snapped into action.

When his crew was on their knees, Christopher nodded to Brambell. Brambell grinned and motioned two of his men who each took one of Christopher's arms and held him tight. Then Brambell swung a fist that connected to Christopher's face painfully. Blood came from his mouth. Christopher stayed on his feet though.

"Go get the girl, and her things," Brambell said to his first mate.

He turned back to Christopher as the man ran up the stairs to the cabin. Brambell continued to hit Christopher as the first mate dragged Celeste from the cabin screaming. When she was on the deck she saw Christopher and broke free to run to him as he fell to his knees, unable to stand.

"Oh, James!" she wrapped her hands around his head as tears fell from her eyes, "Please don't let them take me!"

"I'm sorry, love," he managed to get the words out before

he coughed and more blood came from his mouth.

Then Brambell's first mate grabbed her again and dragged her away to the other ship. Once she was locked away and her trunks put aboard, Brambell looked at Christopher with a frown.

"You used me to save face with that girl. She's in love with you."

"How do you think I got her on my ship," Christopher said with a slight smile.

Brambell grinned, "Good thinking." Then he slammed his fist into Christopher's face once more before leaving.

Christopher lay on the deck until Henry and Robert came and carried him to his cabin. They laid him on the bed carefully before Robert walked to the desk and pulled out a bottle of rum.

"Apply this to his wounds" Robert ordered Henry as he grabbed a shirt from the closet. Henry soaked it in rum and touched it gingerly to a gash on Christopher's brow.

"I'll start us on a course to the port in Florida," Robert said as he walked toward the door.

Christopher could feel someone wiping his face with a wet rag. He could still taste the blood in his mouth, and his head pounded. He tried to open his eyes but he just looked through the slits his eyes made.

"Henry?" he asked when he thought he saw his friend.

"Yes, it's me. Hold still, you're getting blood everywhere. I'm trying to stop it."

Christopher groaned as Henry wiped the rag on his nose.

"Billy's at the helm."

"Where?"

"We're headed for the port in Florida as we planned."

"Good."

"Your eyes are kind of swollen right now. Just rest. I've almost got the blood stopped."

"Why do you sound so happy? Are you smiling?"

"Yes, I am. You deserved this beating, and I think you knew it when you told Brambell to do it. He just beat you more than you thought he would."

"I'm glad you enjoyed it."

"I didn't say I enjoyed it. I thought he was going to kill you for sure. I wasn't so sure he hadn't. I'd say Brambell is the one who enjoyed it. He'll probably gladly do it to you every time."

Christopher groaned again as he felt the bruise on his ribs.

"We should get a doctor to look at you when we get to port." Henry took the rag from Christopher's nose and found the blood had stopped.

"I'll be fine. I just need a drink."

"I figured you'd say that. Should help with the pain." Henry put the bottle in his hand.

Christopher tried to sit up and found his head pounding more while doing so. But he managed to sit up with his back against the wall. The first drink burned the cut on his lip. The second took away the pain.

"Get some rest. Robert's got everything under control." Henry stood and put the chair back over by the desk.

"Thank you, Henry."

Henry smiled, "You're welcome brother."

Chapter 12

Henry, Christopher, Robert, Cale, and Pierre walked along the docks to a tavern. When they arrived they found a table and settled down. It had been a long trip and they were hungry for anything besides rations, with some ale to wash it down.

Suddenly from the kitchen, a short, red-haired young woman came out carrying plates to another table. Henry's attention was drawn to her immediately and couldn't seem to look away. She looked tired, but she was beautiful. Her red hair lay straight down her back, and he suddenly had the longing to see if it was as soft as it looked.

Someone shoved his shoulder.

"What are you staring at, Liam?" Cale asked with a grin.

Henry shook his head like he hadn't been caught watching her. "Nothing."

"She doesn't look like nothing," Cale goaded.

"She is quite lovely," Pierre said with a smirk. "Maybe you should talk to her."

Henry looked at him with exasperation, "Why would I do that?"

"Because she's a woman and you need one," Pierre said with a grin.

"I doubt she'd want to talk to me," Henry shook his head, "And I'm not looking for a woman."

"Well, now is a good time to look. Our pretty captain here doesn't look his best, so you have the chance now." Pierre laughed at Christopher's expense and Christopher just smirked. "Now is your chance," Pierre repeated as he quieted.

"What can I get for you sailors?" a sweet voice came from

over his shoulder and Henry turned to look up into the sea-green eyes of the young woman.

She didn't smile, just waited. He glanced around the table and they all looked at him to answer, and he looked back at her.

"Food and ale, please," he said respectfully.

"Alright," she said as she turned and walked away.

The table of men erupted with laughter, except for Henry who blushed and ducked his head. Cale slapped him on the back.

"See? You did just fine. Now we just need to get her to stick around for you," Cale said grinning.

"I don't think so."

"She'll stay for him," Pierre said, still grinning.

"She's interested in him, she's looked at him four times since we sat down," Robert said.

"She has?" Henry asked as he looked at her again.

They all laughed at him again and he shook his head in irritation with them.

She came over with mugs of ale and gave them each one, saving Henry for last. Their eyes met and he felt himself warm.

"Your food will be ready soon," she said with a slight smile.

He couldn't help but smile back at her a little, "Thank you."

Then she left and the men laughed again.

They spent the evening eating, drinking, and harassing Henry every time the young woman came over. Every time she brought them food and ale she made a point to talk to Henry only. By the end of the evening, she was smiling at him and he didn't care what his mates said. She was beautiful and he couldn't resist smiling back at her.

It was getting late when Robert and Cale decided to leave, and it was only the three of them left.

Suddenly they heard a loud crash from the kitchen and then yelling, and another sound that Henry couldn't make out. Soon the girl came back with a pitcher of ale, and her face was red on one side. Henry frowned as he realized she had been slapped, and her smile wasn't the same.

"This is your last round. My boss is closing up for the night." She looked at Henry and he could tell she was struggling to smile at him. "Can I get you anything else tonight?"

"We're fine, thank you," Christopher answered for him.

The girl looked at Christopher and then back at Henry. "If you change your mind just tell me." Then she walked away, back to the kitchen.

"She wasn't offering him ale," Pierre said to Christopher.

"I know what she was offering. Liam isn't that kind of man," Christopher said as he drank the last of his ale. "Let's go."

"But, captain, he has a wench he likes. You can't make him say no to her. He should decide," Pierre argued.

Christopher looked from Pierre to Henry.

"Are you coming, Liam?" Christopher more commanded than asked as he stood up.

Henry looked at his mug of ale and then back at Christopher, "No, I'm staying for now."

"Liam…"

"Go, James. I'll be back soon."

Christopher shook his head, but walked out of the tavern, with Pierre grinning as he walked out with him.

Henry sat alone and she came back over to lean against the table.

"Would you like to pay for my time, sailor?" she asked with a smile that didn't quite reach her eyes.

"Actually I was hoping we could talk," Henry said as he picked up her hand and caressed it with his thumb.

"I have to work. Either you pay for time with me, or I'll find someone who will," she said sternly.

"I'll pay," he said kindly.

"I have to tell my boss so he knows I'm going upstairs," she said as she pushed away from the table. "I'll be right back."

She went to the kitchen and soon came back. "Alright," she waved her hand, and he stood. She led him upstairs to a room and he walked in. She shut and locked the door.

"Sit on the bed," she ordered and he obeyed.

She started to undo her buttons and he quickly stood again to stop her.

"I told you all I wanted was to talk," he said gently as he took her hands and pulled her to the bed. "Sit," he said as he sat.

"No man just wants to talk," she said, looking at him like he was strange.

He smiled, "I do. I want to know more about you."

She didn't respond except to look at him with concern.

"I promise I'm telling the truth. Look, let's start simple. I'm Henry. What's your name?" he asked.

"Lydia," she said slowly.

"Lydia, that's pretty."

Silence came between them and Henry couldn't help but think of her as a small bird that needed help.

"I'm from Virginia," he offered, "Are you from here?"

Lydia nodded slowly, "Yes, my mother used to work for a lady who had her keeping house."

"Used too?"

"Yes, she died a couple of years ago."

"And you've been working here since?"

"I tried to get work elsewhere but I couldn't. I was hungry and Asher took me in."

"Is he the one who slapped you tonight?" Henry asked as he gently touched the spot on her face.

"Yes, he has a temper. I dropped a plate."

"Does he do that a lot? Hit you I mean."

"He's mean but I'm still alive. Have a roof over my head, food, and work."

"No one deserves to live with someone looming over them like that. My friend's father beat him when he was drinking. And he drank most of the time."

"And you think I need saving, is that it?" she looked at him defensively.

"I'm not thinking anything except that I want to know you more," he gently pushed her hair back from her face. "Have you tried to find somewhere better to work?"

She shook her head, "He doesn't let me go out without him."

Henry frowned, "So you're a prisoner."

She shrugged and looked down at her hands. He reached over and gently took her chin and turned her face to look at him.

"You deserve better."

She shook her head, "There's nothing better for me."

"Tell me what you would do if you could leave." He moved onto the bed until his back was leaning against the wall.

She smiled and moved to do the same.

"I'd move north and find a farm to live on. Grow a garden full of vegetables. Have chickens, and a cow."

Henry grinned, "That sounds nice."

"Would you ever want to stop sailing, Henry?"

Henry thought for a moment, "Maybe someday. It's not turned out the way I dreamed of when I was a child."

She leaned her head on his shoulder and he put his arm around her. "What did you dream it would be?"

They talked for more than an hour before Lydia grew tired and her eyes could barely stay open. Henry realized she was tired when she yawned.

"I should go so you can rest," he said as he moved to the edge of the bed.

"Please don't go," she said, pulling on his arm, "Just sleep here tonight."

She laid down and pulled his arm to lie down next to her. He complied and she laid her head on his chest. He wrapped his arm around her protectively. She soon stopped moving and her breathing slowed. He pushed a piece of her hair from her face with his free hand. She felt good lying next to him. He rested his chin on her head and closed his eyes.

∞∞∞

Henry was startled awake by movement. He opened his eyes to find Lydia looking up at him sweetly and he smiled.

"Good morning, sailor," she said with a smile.

"Good morning," he said softly.

"I have to get up soon to do my chores," she said as she snuggled closer to him.

He turned onto his side and pulled her close.

"Or, we could just stay here all day," he said as he rested his forehead on hers.

She smiled, "I wish we could, but you don't have enough money to pay for my work."

He grinned, "I guess I'll just have to come back tonight."

"You'd come back?" she looked at him with awe.

"Of course." He kissed her nose softly, "May I?"

"I'd love that," she said with a smile that made him feel like the sun was shining through her lovely face.

He caressed her cheek for a moment and then leaned over to kiss her gently. Slowly she kissed him back and it was sweet.

A sudden banging on the door startled them and Lydia sat straight up.

"Get up, girl. You've got chores to do," the voice yelled.

Lydia got up quickly and went to the small mirror on the wall and proceeded to fix her red hair up in a bun.

Henry stood up and leaned against the door, watching her. She saw him in the mirror and smiled.

"You can go, Henry."

"It's hard to leave when I'm looking at the most beautiful woman on the earth," he said with a grin.

She shook her head in exasperation, "You're just saying that."

"Why would I do that?" he frowned a little.

Lydia stopped and looked at him, surprised. "I don't know. I guess you wouldn't."

She walked over to him and put her hands on his chest. "But you really should go. He might not like that I let you stay all night."

"Alright, I don't want to get you in trouble. I'll see you tonight," he said and started to open the door.

"Henry, wait," Lydia caught his arm. She kissed him sweetly. "Goodbye."

With that Henry slipped from the tavern without encountering her boss. He walked down the street to the docks, happily grinning and greeting strangers as he went. When he reached the ship he climbed aboard and went to Christopher's cabin. Henry leaned against the doorway and watched as his friend put on his boots.

"Good morning," Henry said happily.

Christopher looked up with surprise. "Are you just now getting back on board?"

"Yes," Henry said, smiling.

"You stayed at the tavern?"

"Yes, but not the way you're thinking."

"Oh?"

"We talked until we fell asleep. She's smart and interesting. She's beautiful. I'm going back to see her tonight."

Christopher looked at him with sympathy. "I'm sorry, friend, but you have watch tonight."

Henry's smile died, "Oh come on, Chris. I'll take the day shift. Let me go tonight. I can't see her during the day!"

"You'll have to talk to Robert."

Henry walked out of the cabin immediately to find Robert.

Henry was grateful when Robert let him trade with Billy on watch. He walked into the tavern that night with his mates, and they sat at the same table.

Lydia came from the kitchen and smiled when she saw

Henry. He smiled in return but as she came towards him, his smile shifted to anger. He stood quickly and went to her.

"What happened?" He inspected the gash on her cheek.

"It's not bad. I've had worse," she said as she looked up at him with awe at his care.

"I'll kill him myself." Henry started to step around her but she caught his arm.

"No, stop!"

He turned to frown at her.

"You'll just make it worse. Please. Sit down and I'll get you all something to drink. I'm fine," she pleaded with him and he slowly gave in.

"Alright, but I'd be happy to dispose of him for you," Henry said darkly.

She smiled up at him, "Thank you."

"Liam, let the wench get us something to drink already," Pierre interrupted.

Henry turned to glare at Pierre. "Don't call her that," he said firmly.

"It's alright," she squeezed his arm, "I'll get your drinks."

She left and Henry sat back down, still glaring at Pierre.

"Don't tell me you fell for her? You're not supposed to fall for the wenches, Liam," Pierre grinned.

"Leave him alone, Pierre," Christopher ordered. "And don't call her a wench again."

"Yes, captain," Pierre complied but didn't stop grinning at Henry.

"Relax, Liam," Christopher ordered.

Henry looked at him with less animosity than he'd had for Pierre.

"Here you are," Lydia set mugs of ale on the table for each of them. She smiled at Henry and he tried to smile back at her. She leaned down and kissed him softly. "I'll get you something to eat."

"Thank you," he said softly before she backed away and went back to the kitchen.

"Looks like you're going to have to learn how to write letters," Cale said with a grin.

Pierre scoffed and the conversation turned to talk about the cargo on the ship. But Henry stared off thoughtfully and Christopher noticed. He leaned close to Henry.

"What are you thinking?" Christopher talked low so as to not draw attention from the others.

Henry looked at him seriously, "She's in danger here. She needs to get out. We could help her…"

"No," Christopher shook his head, "We can't take her with us. We are headed back to Europe and you know what we're going for. Not to mention a woman on a pirate ship is just asking for trouble, so no. Don't even ask."

"Can we just take her up to Carolsport before we head to Europe? It won't be that far. I'll just take her to my family. She can stay with them, and start a new life."

"No," Christopher was shaking his head again. "We just can't. Brambell is going to be waiting for us, we don't have time for another stop. Besides, what are you going to do when you meet another woman like her who needs the same kind of help? Are you going to rescue them all?"

"No, but Lydia is an angel. She just needs someone to help her get out."

Christopher shook his head yet again, "You're getting too involved."

Henry sat back with irritation. "If she was Joanna, you wouldn't let her stay here with that monster."

"She's not Joanna," Christopher took a drink of his ale.

"You just don't care about a woman enough to do right by her do you?" Henry said accusingly.

Christopher glared at Henry now. "You don't know everything about me."

"Oh? You left Sophie without so much as a look back. You gave Celeste to Brambell without a qualm. You broke Joanna's heart, and you don't seem too upset about any of them."

"As I said, you don't know me as well as you think,"

Christopher said darkly. "Do what you want. I don't care what you do. I was just trying to keep you from making a mistake." He straightened and took a drink of ale.

Henry grew thoughtful. Christopher just didn't know Lydia. He didn't know her sweetness. But there just had to be something he could do for her.

He spent the night with Lydia again talking, and the next night as well. They talked about their dreams and what they would do if life was different. Henry found himself wishing he could do everything they said and more. His feelings for her grew stronger every minute they were together. He wanted nothing more than to help her plant her garden and tend her chickens.

The next morning he had made up his mind and went to find Christopher.

"Please, Chris. I've never asked for anything from you before. I've always been there for you even if I didn't like what you did. And I'll pay you back."

"I think you're wasting your money." Christopher looked back down at his paper as he checked it while the men loaded the cargo. "I let you get away with doing whatever you want, Henry, just because you're my brother. But I don't think you should do this. Stay out of it. Let her go."

"I can't do that. I love her."

Christopher looked at him intently. "Enough to leave the ship?"

Henry looked at him seriously. "You know I wouldn't leave until you did, but yes. I'd gladly stay on land with her. Please loan me the money so I can send her home to my family. They can take care of her and give her the life she deserves."

"What makes you think they will take her in? They don't know her, and your father certainly won't understand."

Henry paused for a moment before saying, "I'm going to marry her before I send her away."

Christopher looked at Henry sharply. "Henry, you can't do that."

"You can't tell me what to do. It's my decision. Someday, I believe we will leave this ship, and I plan to be with her when I do." Henry sounded more confident. "I just need the money to buy her freedom and send her home."

Christopher put his hand on Henry's shoulder, "Henry, please don't do this."

"I'll do it however I have to. If you don't give me the money, I'll find someone who will."

Christopher sighed at the determination in his friend's eyes.

"Alright, I'll give you all you need."

Henry grinned, "Thank you, brother."

"Now get to work, or I'll..."

Henry laughed, "You won't do anything." Then he walked away grinning and went to work.

Christopher shook his head with amusement. Henry was right. He could do whatever he wanted and Christopher wouldn't do anything about it. Henry was loyal, and that's all Christopher needed to know to count on his friend taking his orders. If there was a God, he'd thank Him for Henry, his brother.

"Marry me, and let me send you home to my family," Henry said with a grin. "Someday I'll stop sailing, and come home to you. We'll buy a little farm and you can do whatever you want on it."

Lydia looked at him in awe, "Why would you do that for me?"

"Because I love you. I want to take care of you. I'll send you money so you have what you need. But I know my mother will love you. My father can't turn away my own wife. He'll take you in because you need them. I'm sure they will. And I'll come to you as soon as I can. I'll convince the captain to bring our next cargo shipment to Carolsport and if he doesn't I'll find another way to come see you. I promise."

Lydia smiled at him but tears came to her eyes. "I can't. Asher won't let me leave."

"I'll buy your freedom from him. And if that doesn't work we'll sneak away."

Lydia's eyes widened, "If he catches us he'll kill you, and beat me."

"I can handle myself." He pushed a strand of her hair behind her ear before he leaned in to kiss her. "Please say yes."

Lydia nodded happily, "Yes, yes I'll marry you, Henry."

He picked her up and swung her around. Then he put her down and kissed her again.

"Is your boss still awake? We should ask him tonight. I leave in just a couple of days. There's a ship leaving tomorrow night that is headed north. The port they are going to is only a day's drive to Carolsport. I'll send you with money and directions to my family's home." He kissed her again, and smiled at her with love in his eyes. "We'll get married tomorrow before you get on the ship."

"Everything is happening so fast," she said with wide eyes, "Are you sure we can do this?"

"I'm sure," he rested his forehead on hers gently, "Trust me."

"I do trust you, Henry," she said softly.

"Then I'll go talk to Asher."

Henry made his way downstairs to the kitchen and asked Asher for Lydia's release.

"No! She's not go'n anywhere! She's mine!" Asher yelled. He was drunk and Henry could see there was little chance he'd get any reasonable deal from him. Henry had to try though.

"I'll pay for her freedom."

"You can't afford her!" the man bellowed before taking another drink. "Now get out!"

Henry turned and walked back to Lydia's room. She was

sitting on the bed crying, and he went over and sat next to her. He pulled her into his arms and kissed her head.

"It's alright. We'll just have to sneak you out." He kissed her head again and released her. "Now pack what you can carry, and we'll get you out of here."

She grabbed a small bag and started putting a dress and a few other things in it.

"I don't have much," she said as she finished.

Henry took the blanket off her bed and folded it.

"You'll need this on the ship," he said as he added it to her bag.

Then he grabbed her hand and pulled her towards the door. But when they opened it they found Asher standing outside with a sword in his hand.

"I said you're not taking her anywhere, boy!"

The man slashed the sword towards Henry and Henry sidestepped it. Henry pushed Lydia back and she fell onto the bed. Then Henry pulled his own sword out and raised it. The two fought as their swords clanged together. Henry found Asher more of a challenge than he'd thought, but Asher grew weaker the longer they fought, due to his drunken state, and Henry kept pressing him back. Finally, Asher moved just to the right and Henry pointed his sword towards the man's chest and put his weight into the jab. The sword went directly into Asher's heart and he slowly sunk to the ground as his sword dropped to the floor.

Henry stared at the man lying dead on the floor with shock as blood flowed in a pool away from Asher. He had killed him! He had really just killed him? Mixed feelings started to well up in him but he didn't have time to dwell on them. Lydia was crying and he put his sword away in his belt before grabbing her hand and her bag, and leading her out of the tavern into the night.

They found a place to stay the night and Henry held Lydia tight as he soothed her fears with his calming voice. She finally fell asleep in his arms, with tears dried on her face. Henry stared at the ceiling as he thought about what had happened. The guilt came like a rock in his gut as he thought of having taken a man's life away from him. He felt the tears come to his eyes and he wiped them away, but he felt like he'd been the one to have a sword stuck in his heart.

"What have I done?" he thought over and over until his mind and body grew too tired to stay awake.

∞∞∞

"The house is over here," Henry led Lydia down a street and they came to a stop in front of a small white house. Henry knocked on the door, and it was soon opened by an older gentleman. "Hello, sir, I talked to you yesterday. You said you'd marry me and my girl."

The man smiled, "Come in, son."

They followed the man into the neat, clean house.

"Would you like to go to the church?" the man asked.

"We don't have time, pastor. We have to catch a ship leaving soon," Henry explained.

The man walked to a small table and picked up a bible before walking back to them.

"Please join hands."

Henry and Lydia joined their hands and stood looking at one another.

"What are your names please?"

"I'm Henry Johnson, and this is Lydia."

"Henry, do you take Lydia to be your wife? Forever loving her and forsaking all others?"

"Yes, sir," Henry said with a smile.

Lydia smiled back at him.

"Miss Lydia, do you take Henry as your husband? Forever loving him and forsaking all others?"

"I do, sir," she answered happily.

"By the power vested in me by God, I pronounce you husband and wife. You may kiss your bride."

Henry put his hand on Lydia's face, gently pulling her to him, and kissed her. When he released her she was smiling at him and his heart swelled with joy.

Henry turned to the pastor, "Thank you, sir, we'll be going."

"First, I have something for you." The pastor held out the bible to Henry. "For the family you have just started."

"I couldn't take that, sir," Henry protested.

"I give one to those I marry. It's my gift, so that they may feed their family with the word of God, and grow in His love for them."

Henry wasn't sure why he did, but he took the bible from the pastor, "Thank you, sir."

They left the pastor's home and walked back to the little place where they had stayed. Henry retrieved Lydia's bag and put a small pouch with money into it. He held her hand as they walked towards the docks.

"Now, I found out a small family is traveling on the ship with you. I'm sure they will be good company, and the captain himself promised to help you find someone to take you to Carolsport when you arrive."

Lydia nodded, "Alright." She looked at him longingly, "I wish you could come with me."

He looked at her seriously, "I know, but I can't right now. I will come see you soon."

She nodded.

He smiled at her, "I'll bring you a present too."

Lydia smiled, "I don't need a present, Henry, I just want you."

Henry stopped and turned to her, "I'll bring one anyway."

"As long as you bring it yourself," tears welled up in her eyes and started to fall down her cheek.

"I promise," he said softly as he caught a tear with his finger. Then he started walking again to keep his own emotions from showing.

They walked in silence until they reached the dock of the ship she was to board. They found a man who put her bag on board for her. Then Henry turned to her and took her in his arms to kiss her. The taste of her tears mixed with their kisses and he stopped to look at her.

"I just got you in my life, and now we have to leave each other," Lydia cried softly.

"I know," Henry pulled her into his embrace tightly, "I'm sorry, my love."

"I love you, Henry," She said softly.

"I love you too," he kissed her head.

"Time to go, miss," a sailor said behind them.

Henry pulled away from her and took two papers out of his pocket.

"Here's a letter for you to give to my parents when you get there. It'll explain everything to them. The other paper is directions to the house for when you get to Carolsport. Or you can ask someone how to find Pastor Johnson's house. Most anyone could probably tell you."

Lydia nodded, "Alright."

"I love you," Henry kissed her again and then released her. "Go," he ordered gently.

"Goodbye," she turned and went to the sailor waiting for her.

The sailor helped her on board the ship and then she stood at the railing, looking down at Henry. The ship started to move away from the dock and Henry waved to her. She blew him a kiss and they watched each other until the ship was out of the harbor.

Henry walked slowly back to the Maria. He felt incredibly lonely all of a sudden. He looked down to see the bible still in his hand. He'd have to hide it in his things so the others wouldn't know he had it. They'd just make fun of him for it and maybe grow suspicious being as how he was supposed to be a lawless pirate now. As he climbed back aboard the Maria, he hid it in his vest. He went down to the lower deck and hid it under his blanket.

When he was back up on the upper deck he saw Christopher standing by the helm. He made his way up to the top deck and over to his friend.

Christopher looked at him and nodded, "Did you do what you needed to?"

"She was on the ship that just sailed out," Henry confirmed. Then Henry held out his hand to Christopher, "Thank you, Chris, for helping me."

Christopher shook his hand, "You're welcome. Do you think she'll make it home alright?"

Henry nodded, "Yes, the captain said he'd make sure she found a ride to Carolsport when they reached their port. He seems good to his word."

"Good, I hope everything works out to your liking, Henry. I really do."

"Thanks, Chris. I have a good feeling it will." Henry looked at his feet as he thought about Asher lying dead on the floor. Did he even deserve happiness after killing Asher?

"What's wrong?"

Henry looked up and saw Christopher frowning at him. Henry shook his head and shrugged nonchalantly.

"Nothing. Everything is fine." Henry turned and walked away before he gave away what he was thinking to his best friend.

Chapter 13

They made it to Plymouth, England without incident, and Christopher started asking around about passengers needing to go to the Americas. It took a couple of days until he found a pastor who was headed to the Caribbean to tutor the children of a wealthy family. This sounded as good as any other mark, and it was all he had, so he sent the invitation to the man for a ship to sail on.

"You don't see a problem with taking a pastor to Brambell?" Henry asked as though Christopher had lost his mind. "It's bad enough we gave him that woman. Now we're giving him a man of God?"

"Really, Henry? I handed Celeste over to Brambell and you're asking me if I'm willing to hand over a pastor? I don't see the difference," Christopher frowned at Henry, "Since when do you care? I thought you didn't believe in God."

"I never said I didn't believe He was there. I just didn't care. I still don't think it's right though. What if it brings God's wrath or something down on the ship?"

"You don't believe in that stuff do you?" Christopher smirked at Henry.

Henry shrugged, "It can't hurt to be safe."

"Yes, it can if it doesn't get us paid, and in good with Brambell."

Henry shook his head, "I don't think this is a good idea."

"I didn't ask you if it was a good idea. Now get out and load that new cargo."

"Yes, sir," Henry said sarcastically, which got him a glare from Christopher as Henry walked out the door.

What Henry didn't tell Christopher was that he'd been reading the bible he'd been given and it was giving him a conscience. The man he killed when he saved Lydia haunted his dreams each night.

It felt like a terrible idea to take a man of God to a pirate like Brambell. What would Brambell do to him? Whatever Brambell did would be on their heads. And his hands already had blood on them. Adding more made him feel disgusted. He picked up a small crate and tried not to throw it in anger, down to Pierre.

"What's wrong with you?" Pierre asked as he barely caught the crate.

"Nothing," Henry lied.

∞∞∞

"Welcome aboard the Maria, Pastor Hudson," Christopher said as he gave the man a hand onto the ship.

"Thank you, captain," the pastor said as he looked around. "You have a fine-looking ship, sir."

"Thank you, pastor. If you follow me, I'll show you to your cabin." Christopher led the way up to his cabin and opened the door.

"I don't wish to take your cabin, captain. I don't mind staying below. I'm looking for no special treatment."

Christopher smiled pleasantly, "It's alright, pastor. I certainly don't mind. I'd like you to be comfortable, you're my guest."

"Well, that's very kind of you, sir."

"If you don't mind, I'll continue to use my desk during the day."

"Of course, captain. I'll try not to disturb you while you work."

"I'm sure we'll be just fine," Christopher nodded, "I'll let you settle in. If you excuse me, I must get us underway."

"Thank you, captain."

Christopher left and walked up to the top deck and stood next to Henry, who waited at the helm.

"Cob, get us going," Christopher ordered Robert who in turn started ordering men to set sail, and soon the ship began to sail out of the harbor.

Christopher looked at Henry, but Henry stared straight ahead.

"Still mad at me for sailing with him on board?"

"Nothing wrong with sailing with the good pastor. It's what we're going to do with him that's wrong. God's going to punish us."

Christopher shook his head with a smirk of amusement, "When did you start to care so much?"

Henry looked at Christopher and then back at the waters ahead.

"The pastor who married Lydia and I gave me a bible as a wedding present. I've been reading it when I didn't have anything better to do. I don't understand most of it, but it has some interesting stories I don't remember reading before."

Christopher looked at him like he'd gone mad. Henry glanced at him and grew embarrassed.

"I shouldn't have told you," Henry shook his head.

"I don't care that you're reading it. Just don't let it get in the way of our operations."

"So you wouldn't mind if I talk to the pastor when I'm not on duty?"

Christopher continued to look at Henry like he was insane, "I don't care what you do off duty, just don't start preaching to the crew."

"Thanks," Henry said before going back to his work quietly.

Christopher wasn't sure what to think about Henry's reading the bible. Henry had always thought church and the bible were boring and a waste of time. He'd been forced to listen to his father preach at home, as well as at church. Henry used to complain about sitting through such times. He'd talk of freedom to do anything he wanted and not have to listen to his father's sermons again. So why the sudden interest in the bible now?

Henry hadn't been the same since he met Lydia in Florida. Something was different but Christopher couldn't figure out what, and Henry wasn't volunteering anything. He was just going to have to come out and ask him.

"Henry, did something happen in Florida when you went to take Lydia to the ship? You left the evening previous quite content and jolly, but haven't been yourself since you came back. Do you miss her that much, or did something happen?"

Henry was silent for a moment, and Christopher waited.

"I killed Lydia's boss at the tavern."

Christopher looked at Henry in shock, "You what?"

"He came at me with a sword. I had to defend myself," Henry said, disgusted, "I won."

Christopher stared at his friend thoughtfully. "I'm sorry I wasn't there to help you."

Henry shrugged, "We're pirates, right?"

Christopher didn't say anymore, but he knew his friend wasn't a pirate at heart. He was a good man, and he needed out.

"I heard you spent all your money while in England. I guess you won't be paying me back any time soon," Christopher smirked, "What did you spend so much money on?"

Henry reached into his pocket and pulled out a small gold ring with a small ruby on it that almost looked like a teardrop.

"For Lydia."

Christopher took it and looked at it closely before handing it back, "Looks nice."

"Do you think she'll like it?" Henry frowned slightly, "It's not very big."

"I think if she loves you as much as you love her, then she'll like anything you give her."

Henry smiled, "Thanks, Chris."

Then Henry became quiet again for a moment.

"Chris, where were you planning to go after we meet up with Brambell?"

Christopher shrugged, "Just to the nearest port. The cargo we have can go just about anywhere really. Why?"

"Could we go home so I can see Lydia? I want to make sure she made it alright."

Christopher didn't like the idea of going home now that he knew Joanna wouldn't want to see him. But he knew Henry needed to, and maybe he could convince his friend to stay home with his family. Surely he could do that for Henry after all he'd put up with from Christopher. He would just stay on the ship or go to the tavern, and stay away from Joanna.

"Alright. We'll go."

Henry grinned, "Thank you, brother."

Christopher smiled slightly before turning away to talk to Robert.

∞∞∞

A knock on the cabin door pulled Christopher's attention from his papers.

"Come in."

The door opened to Henry who nodded to the pastor when Christopher looked at him.

"Pastor, this is my friend, Liam. If you'll excuse me, I'll say good night," Christopher put away his papers and took a bottle of rum out of the desk before he left the cabin.

The pastor looked at Henry and smiled, "Hello, Liam."

"I hope I'm not disturbing you. I know it's starting to get late, but I just got off my watch." Henry stepped in and closed the door.

"Not at all, son. Do come in. Is there something I can do for you?"

"Yes, sir," Henry nervously took a chair and moved to sit

in it next to the bed where the pastor sat. "The man who married me and my wife gave me this." Henry pulled the bible from inside his vest. "I've been reading, but I don't understand some of it. My father is a pastor as well, but I never cared much about the bible growing up. I'd like to understand a few things now though."

"That's alright, son. God reveals His truths to us a few at a time. He knows we'd be overwhelmed to have them all at once." The older man smiled kindly, "But why don't you show me what you are reading and what your question is. Maybe I can help you."

"I've been reading about how God demanded sacrifices from the Israelites, but I don't understand why God would ask them to do that."

The pastor nodded, "That does seem like an odd thing to ask of people, doesn't it? The sacrifices were a way for a person to realize their accountability for their sins. To show them the blood that was on their hands. To help them understand what they had done was wrong. We all have to be held accountable for the things we do wrong in our lives. We don't have a visual like the sacrifices today. That's why we must realize our sins and seek to be forgiven in a new way."

"You mean through Christ. My father used to preach a lot about Christ dying for our sins."

"Yes, He has died unblemished to save us. Why don't you read the gospel of John, and when you have done that I'll give you some more verses to read. Then we can talk about them."

Henry nodded, "Alright."

"Tomorrow I'll borrow some paper from the good captain and write down the verses for you."

"Yes, sir, thank you," Henry rose and set the chair back by the desk, "Good night, sir."

"Good night, Liam."

∞∞∞

"Are you reading again? This is the third night in a row." Christopher sat down next to Henry and held out the bottle in his hand. "Have a drink with me, Henry."

"Not now, Chris," Henry looked at him.

"Fine." Christopher sat back against the wall and took a drink before asking, "What are you reading about anyway?"

"About Christ. I'm just getting to the part about the Romans who are killing him." Henry glanced at Christopher and then read out loud, "'Then Pilate therefore took Jesus, and scourged him. And the soldiers platted a crown of thorns and put it on his head, and they put on him a purple robe, And said, Hail, King of the Jews! and they smote him with their hands.' Then Pilate tries to get the people to let Jesus go, but they won't. So he condemns him to be crucified."

Henry glanced at Christopher and saw that he was listening, so he continued to explain.

"So they drove nails into his hands and feet, nailing him to the wood." Henry grimaced, "Then Jesus died as his mother and disciples watched."

Christopher sat thinking about what Henry read and then took another drink.

"What do you think?"

"Sounds like a horrible way to die." Christopher stood and walked away, but the words seemed to go with him. He couldn't shake the feeling that he had been the one to do all those things to an innocent man. He took another drink and willed the intrusive thoughts to go away as he sat down next to Pierre to listen to a different story.

"The good pastor comes up every day while I'm at the helm," Henry said as he held the helm firmly. Christopher was standing next to him with a chart in his hands.

"So?"

"He's from London. Grew up in a wealthy family. His older brother was the one who would inherit, and he was happy about that. He said he found God and realized he didn't need material things to be happy. Then he started tutoring other children in the wealthy, in hopes of teaching them to understand the same thing he had realized. He said so many are taught to be spoiled, he wished to give them a better life than that."

"That's noble," Christopher said sarcastically, "And now he's going to the Caribbean, for what?"

"He said he felt God was calling him to help a family friend with his four children. He believes they require God's guidance."

"God called him?" Christopher said skeptically.

"Yes, he said he prays to know God's will for his life. He wants to honor God by obeying Him."

"God talks to him? Doesn't that seem a little far-fetched, Henry?"

"That's what I said. He said God reveals His will at the opportune time so that he knows it's God speaking."

Christopher looked at Henry with impatience. "He speaks to him? Like you and I are talking now?"

"Not exactly. He said sometimes God speaks to him through the bible. Other times God speaks to him through another person. And sometimes God speaks to him when he's praying. God gives the answers he seeks in his thoughts."

Christopher rolled his eyes, "Henry..."

"I know what you're going to say, Chris, but it doesn't seem as far-fetched as you say," Henry shrugged, "It seems like a nice conversation. Not at all like when we had to pray as children."

"A proper pirate doesn't ask such questions, nor dwells on them, Henry. I don't understand why you insist..."

"Because I'm not happy, Chris," Henry's anger surprised Christopher, "Life on this blasted ship hasn't been at all what we thought."

It had been what Christopher had thought it would be. But he knew his friend was too good for the life of a pirate.

"I'm sorry, Henry," he said softly, "I think when we get to Carolsport, you should stay there."

Henry looked at him slightly surprised, "What about you?"

"I'll be fine, Henry," Christopher tried to sound firm, but he knew he'd miss his friend more than he could say. "I want you to be happy. You should stay home with Lydia and your family."

"Thank you, Chris, but I don't think I could leave you alone."

"You'll do fine without me. Better without me actually."

"Chris..."

"What else has the pastor been telling you?" He didn't really care, he just wanted to get Henry to stop arguing with him.

"Well, I told him that I read the book of John, you know the one I read to you the other night."

"Yes?"

"He said a man put sin between mankind and God, and only a man could bring us back to God. Jesus was perfect. He was like a clean lamb. No blemish was in his heart. He was sinless. If anyone deserved to live forever, it was him. But He knew the only way to bring mankind back to God was to offer himself as a sacrifice for the sins of the world. And that's exactly what He did. He died to take away the sins of the world. Yours and mine alike."

"Why would he do that?"

"Because He loves us. Only great love could make such a sacrifice. Evil always does what is best for itself. Love sacrifices self for others. But Jesus made a way for us to overcome our sins. All we have to do is accept His sacrifice of love. Ask Him for forgiveness for our sins, and be baptized into the family of God. When we choose to do this, then we are given true freedom of sin's death."

Henry looked down for a moment, and Christopher could see shame written on his face.

"He asked me if I have sin that I think can never be

forgiven. I thought about having killed Asher when I was taking Lydia away. Then the pastor said even our worst sin can be forgiven by the loving savior. And once He's forgiven us, we can be with the loving God who made us."

"What do you mean freedom from death?" Christopher asked with a frown.

"After Jesus died He was in the grave for three days and then raised from the dead, and taken to heaven to be with His father, God. Someday He will return to earth and create a new kingdom. One that He will rule. When He comes, those who were baptized in Jesus' name, will rise from the dead to join Him in His new kingdom. They will live forever with Him. There will be no more sin, no more sorrow, no more suffering. Those who do not choose Him in this life will be judged by God and thrown into the lake of fire to be consumed. That will be their final death. So the choice is up to us. To choose life forevermore with God and Christ, or to die a horrible death."

Christopher sighed in annoyance, "It doesn't matter in this life what will happen in the next. If I die, I die. I don't think I care if I live forever or not." Then he walked away with the chart rolled up tightly in his hand.

Henry watched his friend walk away. He knew Christopher wouldn't take him seriously. He wasn't even sure why he shared what he'd learned with Christopher. As for himself, the more he read the more he wanted to know. He couldn't help feeling like Jesus was the answer to his problem. The guilt of all he'd done since boarding the ship weighed on him heavily more and more. The idea that Jesus could not only forgive him for those things but also help him find peace, was a tempting offer.

Chapter 14

"We are only a couple of days out. Are you sure you want to do this?" Robert asked him.

Christopher glared at the man, "Why would you ask that?"

Robert shrugged, "The girl was one thing. I was fairly confident she would be kept safe. I'm not as confident about the pastor. Besides, I've seen how Henry has taken to the man. And I know how you are about Henry. You tend to get broody when you know he'll be mad at you for something."

"Henry already knows my mind. If he expects any different he'll have to deal with it." Tell Cale to be on the lookout for Brambell."

"Yes, sir."

When Robert didn't leave, Christopher looked at the man again.

"What?"

"You don't think we're bringing bad luck on us do you?"

"Damn that Henry! I told him not to spread his superstitious ideas." Christopher growled as he shook his head in irritation.

"Henry didn't say anything to me." Robert said with surprise, "Are you saying he's thinking the same thing?"

"In a way." Christopher looked at Robert hard. "Stop with the nonsense and get back to work."

"Yes, sir."

Robert turned and walked away. Christopher frowned as he looked at the chart. He couldn't help feeling that something was going to go very wrong. Were Henry and Robert right? Were they going to bring something bad down on them?

Christopher shook his head. No, they'd be fine. Surely. But the feeling didn't go away. Instead, it nagged at him the rest of the day.

When he went below that evening he immediately looked for a bottle of rum. Then he walked over and sat next to Henry, where he took a long drink before he noticed the look on Henry's face.

"What are you reading now that has you frowning?" Christopher nodded to the paper in Henry's hand.

"The pastor gave me some more verses and he wrote a note. 'Have you been honest with yourself about the things you don't like about yourself? Are there things you've chosen to do that you now regret? Have these things made you a better man, or have you become someone you don't care to see in a mirror anymore?'"

"Those seem like rather judgemental questions," Christopher said with slight irritation.

"I don't think he meant them as such," Henry said thoughtfully. "Does anything you've done bother you? Do you think they are wrong?"

"I'm a pirate, Henry. I can't afford to care if they are wrong or not."

"Yes, but do you feel bad about things you've done?"

Christopher sighed, "Yes, Henry, I do, but I can't dwell on them during times like this. I have to stay in control."

Henry nodded, "I understand. I just can't seem to get Asher out of my head."

"I'm sure it'll dull in time."

"Has it for you?"

Christopher looked at him seriously.,"Not yet. I choose to believe it will though."

Henry nodded, "I hope you're right."

Christopher took another drink before lying down and closing his eyes.

∞∞∞

The next morning he walked up to his cabin and sat at his desk. The pastor was up on the top deck so Christopher was alone. His mind couldn't seem to focus on the work in front of him.

He couldn't help thinking about the questions the pastor had posed to Henry. He'd been trying to avoid thinking of them, but they just kept coming back to him.

He had most certainly thought about the things he'd had to do. Throwing Brack overboard, killing Hunter, whipping Stretch, and giving Celeste to Brambell. It bothered him to know he was giving yet another innocent person to Brambell, but if he didn't, Brambell might kill him. Maybe even the crew as well. Christopher couldn't help but worry and wonder what would happen to Henry if he should die.

He knew Henry wasn't a true pirate. Henry couldn't stand the killing and kidnapping. But what about himself? Celeste haunted him. He thought about her and wondered if she made it home safely. He had hurt her, and the guilt weighed on him.

If he was honest with himself, he didn't like who he'd become.

"Cale just spotted Brambell," Robert said as he walked into the cabin.

Christopher stood quickly and went around the desk. "Take us to him."

The two men went up to the top deck as Robert gave orders to the crew. Christopher went to the helm where he found Henry talking to the pastor.

"Pastor Hudson, I'm afraid you'll have to return to the cabin. Pirates have been spotted and I don't want them to know you're here."

"I understand, sir. I'll pray for things to go with God's

will."

Christopher watched the man walk away and down the stairs. Then he turned to look at Henry.

"You can't do this, Chris," Henry said with a grave expression, "We can still get away."

"No, we can't. His ship is lighter and faster than us. We can't outrun him, and he's already seen us. We've signaled him. It's too late."

Henry shook his head in anger. Christopher tried to ignore him and focus on what his crew was doing as they came closer to Brambell.

Soon they were laying planks across the gap between the two ships. Brambell walked across the planks and stepped onto the Maria with an evil grin.

"I see you've returned. With a prize I hope, that will make me a lot of money."

Christopher held steady, but his conscience about what he was about to do made him ask a question.

"I don't suppose we could come to a different arrangement this once?" he asked quietly.

Brambell walked closer and looked at Christopher with a glare.

"Who do you have?" Brambell asked.

"A pastor who is headed to a family friend. They are wealthy and he's supposed to tutor their children," Christopher said without showing the nervousness he felt.

"Aw, and you don't want to ransom a man of God. How considerate of you, sir," Brambell said sarcastically. "I don't care who it is, as long as he makes me money."

Then Brambell stepped closer and got in Christopher's face.

"Just for asking me that, I'm going to make you get your hands dirty."

Fear dropped in Christopher's gut like a rock at the possible acts that Brambell might force him to do.

Brambell stepped back, "I think a proper pirate should

have a reputation for being a pirate. So, you and one of your men will come with us to ransom the good pastor. Your ship will stay here and wait for you. We'll be gone a week or more. And if you fail to do what I say then I will blow your ship out of the water when we return. You'll watch your ship and your men sink into the depths before I hang you from the mast." Brambell looked around at Christopher's crew for a moment before walking up to Henry and pulling him out of line. "You'll come along to help your captain."

"No!" Christopher looked at Henry with fear. "I'll pick someone to bring."

"You're not in command here. I chose this man, and he will be the one to come." Brambell came back over to Christopher and got in his face before pointing to the cabin. "Now go get my prize."

"Yes, sir," Christopher walked away and went to the cabin. He opened the door and looked at the pastor sternly. "Please come with me, sir."

The pastor didn't even ask what was going on, which surprised Christopher. He just walked with Christopher down to the deck.

"Liam, get the pastor's trunk," Christopher ordered.

"Yes, sir," Henry walked away.

"Captain, I request my crew be allowed to make port while we're away. They will run out of supplies if they stay here." Christopher said to Brambell carefully.

Brambell sneered, "I'll leave them with a few supplies, but not enough. If you want to save your crew, then you'd better hurry with your mission." Brambell walked to the edge of the ship and up to the planks. Then he gestured to his ship. "Shall we?"

Henry came down the stairs with the pastor's small trunk and followed Christopher and the pastor across the planks to Brambell's ship.

"Put all three of them in the hold. Give them one ration each day." Brambell yelled to his crew.

Crewmen came to the three men and grabbed their arms to take them down into the ship. There, they put them in the hold and closed the door. Only a dim light shone in the room and the three men stood silently for a moment.

"I'm sorry, Liam," Christopher crossed his arms and leaned his back against the door.

"I know. Thanks for trying." Henry moved a barrel over towards the pastor, "Here, sir, you can sit on this." The man sat with a grateful smile.

Christopher looked at the pastor curiously. "You don't seem very upset to be taken by pirates."

"I knew something was up by the way you two behaved. You seemed to be arguing and I could tell that only two close men would forgo the captain-to-sailor relationship for something more important. You are brothers?"

Christopher and Henry looked at him slightly surprised.

"Not blood, but yes," Henry said.

Pastor Hudson nodded, "I could tell. I've been praying for you both since I boarded. I do not doubt in my mind that God has great plans for you both. Despite your piracy."

Christopher looked at the floor thoughtfully.

"I'm sorry, sir," Henry said sadly.

"It's alright, son," Pastor Hudson smiled, "I believe the turn in events has been for a reason."

"What reason?" Henry looked at him quizzically.

"So that we could spend more time together, and continue our discussions."

Christopher shook his head slightly in amusement.

"What?" Henry asked Christopher.

"Leave it to the good pastor to find something good to come out of this mess." Christopher slid down to sit in defeat.

"Will the crew be alright?" Henry asked.

"I don't know. I'm sure Cob will ration everything but we'll be pushing the limit when we finally pull into port."

"What if they leave?"

Christopher shook his head, "Cob won't let them. He's too

loyal."

Henry sat down next to him.

"According to the charts I saw, we might be able to go to an island nearby and find some fresh water and maybe some food before we head to port." Christopher leaned back against the wall and closed his eyes. "I can't believe I got us into this mess. And dragging you in with me. I was ready to leave you at home when we went. I wasn't going to let you step foot back on the ship. Now here we are on Brambell's ship, about to make it that much harder for you to leave."

"You know I'd never leave you on the ship without me, James."

"I know. That's why I'd planned to leave while you were at home, without your knowing."

Henry snickered, "What would you do without me?"

"Lose my conscience. I'd probably just do whatever a pirate does. You wouldn't be there to question my every move."

"Sorry."

"Don't be. I'm glad you do." Christopher smiled at Henry.

"So you're saying you have a conscience?" Henry smirked.

Christopher just shook his head in amusement.

A day later the ship stopped at a port and they could hear the sounds of the port, but they weren't allowed out of the hold. Soon they were moving again, but not even a full day had passed when the anchors were lowered. Christopher, Henry, and Pastor Hudson were all taken to the upper deck. They blinked in the bright sunshine. The day was hot and sticky but the breeze felt good. They were forced into a boat with Captain Brambell, his first mate, and four crewmen. They rowed to the shore and Christopher couldn't see anything but a jungle ahead of them.

"Where are we?" he asked curiously.

"This island is where I do my exchanges. It is quiet and secluded, and I've never seen another soul here. Yesterday I sent a man to the good pastor's friend and it should only take them a day or so to get to the meeting spot. By the time we reach the other side of the island tomorrow, they should be there. We have a few good hours of light before we have to stop for the night. We should be able to get at least halfway by then." Brambell jumped out of the boat as it came up to the shore.

Everyone followed and the crewmen pulled the boat up so it wouldn't float away.

"Let's get moving." Brambell led the way, followed by Christopher, the pastor, Henry who carried the pastor's trunk, the first mate, and the other crewmen.

It was slow going through the jungle overgrowth. They were sweating, hot, and thirsty just an hour into the trek.

Christopher looked back to check on the pastor and saw Henry struggling with the trunk. He broke from his place in line and took the trunk from Henry before moving back in front of the pastor.

When it was too dark to walk any further, they stopped and the crewmen made a fire to cook rations over.

"Don't cook too much, they already had their rations today," Brambell told the man who was cooking.

Christopher looked at Henry and the pastor tiredly. He knew they needed those rations. They were tired and weak from not having the food they needed. When they were passed the water, they drank their fill to help their hunger. He could tell the trek was hard on the older pastor. Henry laid down and closed his eyes. Christopher could tell it wouldn't take long for him to be asleep. The others followed, and soon he was listening to snores coming from everyone except the pastor. He looked at the man who sat quietly staring into the fire.

"Henry read a little about Christ dying to me," Christopher said quietly.

The pastor looked at him with a smile. "What did you think?"

"I told Henry it sounded like a terrible way to die."

"It was."

Christopher shrugged with a confused look, "Why would He go through all of that, just to save people who didn't want Him?"

"Let me ask you a question. You love your brother, Liam, right?"

"Yes, sir."

"Would you die for him if it meant he would be saved from death?"

Christopher looked at the pastor with a frown, "Of course."

"Imagine a man who loves every person on the earth so much that He'd lay down his life for them all."

Christopher looked at the pastor with sudden understanding.

"He loved you so much, James, that He died to save you from death. He wants you to be happy. To live a good life full of happy times with those you love."

Christopher shook his head, "But I've not done anything worth saving. Liam is a good man. He deserves love like that."

"He didn't pick and choose who gets saved, son. He chose everyone. He gives everyone the chance to choose Him. It doesn't matter what you've done or will do. He'll love you and wait for you to realize He's there for you. All you have to do is cry out to Him."

A warm feeling moved into Christopher's heart and mind at the thought of someone loving him enough to lay down their life for him. Just as he would gladly do for Henry. But he didn't feel worthy of such love and the feeling lessened.

"Good night, pastor," he said before he laid down and closed his eyes.

"Good night, son."

∞∞∞

The next morning they walked on through the thick jungle. The heat and humidity made their shirts drip with sweat.

Finally, they came out of the jungle to a beach. Henry dropped the trunk in the sand as they all stopped. Christopher bent over and put his hands on his knees to hold himself up. He looked over to see Henry sitting on the sand tiredly. The pastor next to Henry.

"That must be their ship," Brambell said as though he wasn't bothered by the trek at all. "They should see us soon, and send their man in. Until then, we wait."

They didn't have long to wait. They watched as a boat was lowered from the ship, two men got in and started rowing. When they made it to shore they brought a small chest with them.

"Are you Brambell?" one man asked.

"I am. And this is Captain James. He's here to take the money," Brambell said with an evil gleam in his eyes.

The two men looked at Christopher and he went to take the chest from them. Then he gave it to Brambell's first mate.

"Good, take them," Brambell gestured and his crewmen grabbed the two men.

Christopher looked at Brambell with confusion. Brambell walked over to the two men and sliced their throats with his sword. They dropped the men in the sand and Brambell nodded to his crewmen. Immediately, they moved to take Henry and the pastor in their grasp.

"Now, sir," Brambell came over to Christopher, "I promised you you could get your hands dirty on this venture." He pointed to Henry. "I overheard you say last night, that this is your brother."

Christopher felt his heart stop and he looked at Brambell in fear. What did he mean? What could he want with Henry? A sick feeling landed in his gut and he looked at Henry. Henry looked back in surprise. Christopher looked at Brambell who was grinning, and Brambell pointed to Henry.

"You have a choice. You can save your brother and kill the good pastor. Or I'll drown them both myself."

Christopher looked at Henry and then the pastor in horror.

"You can't do this!" Henry yelled.

"Shut up you whelp." Brambell yelled back, "Keep him quiet."

One of the crewmen holding Henry put a rag in his mouth. Brambell clapped a hand on Christopher's shoulder and pushed him towards Henry and the pastor.

Christopher looked at the pastor in terror! How could he possibly do such a thing? The man was innocent. He was a good man. A man of God.

Brambell stopped him just in front of the pastor. The pastor looked straight back at Christopher and that's when Christopher realized the pastor didn't look scared at all. He frowned at the man in confusion.

"It's alright, son. I'm ready to die. You and your brother are not." Pastor Hudson nodded, "Do it."

Christopher stood still, just staring at the man in amazement. Then guilt came seeping into his mind and heart as he realized he had to save Henry. How could he sacrifice one good man for another?

"Last chance, or I start drowning your brother first." Brambell's voice came from behind him and drew him out of his daze.

Trembling, Christopher drew his sword slowly. Tears came to his eyes as guilt and shame swept through him.

"It's alright, son," The pastor whispered back with a nod, "I forgive you."

Christopher stood a moment more as he stared at the pastor in despair. Then he raised his arm and ran his sword into the pastor's heart quickly. He stared straight ahead as the pastor fell off his sword, into the sand.

"Good. I'm glad to see you can take orders again."

Brambell's voice broke the silence.

Anger, shame, and hurt ran through Christopher. He wanted nothing more than to run his sword through Brambell. But he knew he couldn't take on six men. Two of which had knives to Henry's throat.

"Let's be going. We've got to get you back to your ship before your crew dies of thirst."

From the corner of his eye, he saw them release Henry. But Christopher couldn't move. He stared at the dead pastor with pain. He looked at his sword dripping blood and felt like the blood covered him as well. Tears fell from his eyes as he stared at the dead man lying in the sand. He was sickened by the sight. Sickened with himself for putting him there. Sickened by who he'd become. How could he ever make it right?

"Let's go!" yelled Brambell.

Henry's hand touched Christopher's shoulder.

"Let's go, James," he said calmly before turning and walking away.

Christopher turned slowly as he replaced his sword, and started to walk when he noticed the pastor's trunk. He walked over and opened it. He found what he was looking for quickly, and took the Bible from the trunk before closing the lid. He wasn't sure why he wanted it, but he felt he needed it for some reason. He slid the small book into his shirt for safekeeping, and with one look back at the pastor lying in the sand, he turned to catch up to the rest of the men.

Henry thought about the pastor soberly as he lay staring up into the treetops, tears rolling down from his eyes. The man had told Christopher he was ready to die, and they were not. Henry suddenly realized the pastor was right. He wasn't ready to die.

"I'm sorry, Lord. Please forgive me. I don't deserve your forgiveness for what I've done. Please forgive my trespasses. I want to be a better man. Someone worthy of your love. Please show me how to do that." The longer he prayed, the better he began to feel. Like a weight lifted from his shoulders. Then a warmth came to his chest as he thought about the verse he'd read about angels rejoicing when God's children came back to Him. The idea of rejoicing made him smile a little. He wanted to be the reason for rejoicing in heaven. *"I'm going to follow you, Lord. From now on, I will do my best to follow your will. Starting by leaving the ship. Even if that means I have to leave Chris."*

Chapter 15

Christopher stepped down onto his ship and walked away from Brambell's ship as the planks were drawn in.

"Get us to the nearest island and we'll find water and food before we go on," he ordered Robert. Robert moved to give orders to the tired, thirsty, and hungry crew they had returned to.

Brambell's ship started moving away to the south.

Christopher walked to his cabin and shut the door. He took the bible out of his shirt and set it on his desk. He stared at the book for a moment before he started seeing the pastor's dead face again.

Then something broke in him. He backed away from the desk until he hit the wall. Sliding down the wall to sit on the floor, as he started to cry.

"What have I done?" he asked aloud. "What have I done?"

Suddenly Henry and Robert's fears about being punished by God made him suddenly fearful.

"Please don't punish my crew, God! Don't punish them for my sin! I didn't want to do it! I wouldn't have done it! But they were going to kill Henry! I couldn't let them kill Henry, God! Please punish me. Don't punish anyone because of me!"

His heart ached like someone had stabbed him. He reached for his heart but nothing was there. He cried from the pain of guilt until he could hardly breathe.

"I'm sorry. I'm so sorry. Please forgive me. I'm so sorry."

When he finally calmed down he moved to his bed and laid down. He closed his eyes, but all he saw were his victims. He soon fell into a fitful sleep.

∞∞∞

"Captain," Robert's voice came through his nightmares and Christopher sat up quickly.

It took a moment for him to register where he was and that Robert was standing next to his bed.

"What?" he said tiredly as he rubbed his face.

"We found an island and we're anchored nearby. Do you want me to send men to look for food and water?"

"Yes," Christopher nodded.

Robert walked out and closed the door behind him. Christopher got up and changed his clothes. He looked at the bible on his desk for a moment before he opened the door and went outside. He walked out to see tired men getting into row boats. He saw Henry headed to the side of the ship, to join them.

"Liam," Christopher yelled to him and Henry looked up, "You don't have to go."

"Yes, I do," Henry said before he went over the side.

Christopher went up to the top deck and looked at some charts.

"Where will we be headed next?" Robert's voice startled him, and he turned.

"Carolsport," he replied.

Robert looked at him surprised.

"I promised Henry we'd go, and I want to make sure he stays this time."

Robert nodded, "I understand. I'll help any way you need."

"Thank you."

Once they had enough food and water, they set sail again. Christopher walked back down to his cabin and sat down at his desk. He had only been staring at the bible for a few minutes when a knock came on the door. He quickly put the bible inside the desk.

"Yes?"

The door opened to Henry.

"I just needed to tell you something," Henry said quietly.

"Come in."

Henry closed the door and sat down in front of the desk. "Robert said we're headed for Carolsport."

"Yes," Christopher nodded slightly.

"I think I'm ready to leave the ship. I don't think I can live this life anymore. If I hadn't been here, the pastor would still be alive."

Christopher looked at him with surprise, "What?"

"If I hadn't pushed you to keep the pastor safe, then you wouldn't have asked Brambell to change the deal. He wouldn't have made us go with him and you wouldn't have had to kill the pastor. It's all my fault." Henry choked back emotion.

"It's not your fault, Henry. It's entirely mine. If I hadn't gotten us into this whole mess in the first place, then none of this would have happened. But I agree you should go home to stay. You deserve to be happy, Henry. I'll be glad to know you're home safe with Lydia and your family."

"I don't know if I'll ever be happy without you there. Won't you consider staying with me?"

"I'm a lost cause, Henry. There's just too much for me to come back from."

Henry shook his head, "I don't believe that. I believe what the pastor was trying to tell us is true. Jesus loves us and He wants to save us." Henry looked thoughtful for a moment, "I've decided I want to be baptized when I return home."

Christopher looked at Henry with surprise, "You do?"

"Yes," Henry looked more confident, " And I'll pray that you find Him too. I know He wants us, Chris. When we left that beach, I realized I didn't want to live my life without knowing I was ready to die. The pastor said he wasn't afraid because he was ready. We're not ready, Chris. I want to be though. I want to know that if I should die in this life, I will live again in a truly free world. Free of all that is wrong with this world. That's the kind of freedom I want. That's the freedom we've been searching for all this time."

Christopher thought about what Henry was saying but didn't respond.

Henry stood, "My shift is starting. Goodnight, Chris."

"Good night, Henry."

When Henry had closed the door, Christopher opened his desk drawer and pulled out the bible again. He turned through the pages mindlessly at first until he found the book of John.

He opened to the beginning of the book and started reading. It was late into the night when he got to the part about Jesus being beaten and harassed.

He suddenly couldn't help but feel like he was the one beating this innocent man who had done nothing but teach others about love! Suddenly the pastor's face loomed in his forethought.

The feel of his sword cutting through the fabric of the pastor's clothing, and then hitting his rib bones, before piercing his heart. The cold eyes stared up at him from the ground as blood soaked into the sand.

Guilt pierced through Christopher's heart like a knife, and tears came to his eyes. Like the pastor, Jesus had done nothing to deserve death. He had taught about love and respect. Jesus had never done anything to anyone that wasn't right. But he had been brutally beaten and nailed to a cross.

Christopher looked at his hands. He could almost see the blood on them. He didn't just see the blood of his victims of piracy, but also the blood of Jesus Himself! Fear struck him and he closed his eyes. No. He hadn't really done those things to Jesus. How could he? It was another time and place. Yes, he had blood on his hands, but not Jesus' blood! He didn't actually do those things to Him!

But it felt so real. And he suddenly realized that he was no better than the men that really had beaten and crucified the most peaceful and loving human that was ever on the earth.

The pain he felt almost had him slamming the book shut,

but instead, he kept reading. Desperate for there to be hope for him.

Jesus came back to life and went to heaven to be with God, just like Henry had said. It sent a warm feeling through him to know that the story hadn't ended in death. That Jesus lived again. Then he realized that the feeling he was experiencing was the hope he was looking for.

Was Henry right? Could he be saved? Was there hope for him?

What was it Henry had said? That he had to admit his sins and ask Jesus to forgive him? Was it really that simple? He wasn't sure. But what did he have to lose if he didn't try?

"Jesus, I don't know what to say. I know I'm guilty of many things. I hate who I've become, and I regret pulling Henry down with me. I ask for your forgiveness, and I beg your guidance to help me become a better man."

Christopher slowly felt the weight on his shoulders start to lift. Hope slowly warmed his heart and mind. And it felt like someone had whispered into his soul. "I forgive you."

Tears of hope and joy came down his face, and he smiled.

"Thank you, Jesus. Thank you for dying to save me."

He looked at the precious book in front of him and shut it slowly with reverence.

Christopher woke feeling better than he could ever remember. Hope had his spirits high, and he smiled as he got dressed. He walked up to the top deck where he found Henry at the helm, and went to him quickly.

"Liam!"

"James, what's wrong? Why are you smiling?" Henry looked at him with worry.

"Nothing's wrong, Liam I just wanted to tell you, you

were right. Last night when you said I could still be saved. I believe you now."

"You do?" Henry looked at him in surprise.

"Yes, I prayed last night and He really was there to hear my prayers. I truly believe He has forgiven me!"

Henry's grin spread across his face. "That's good news, brother!" Henry held out his hand to Christopher and Christopher shook it. "Does this mean you'll come home with me now?"

Christopher sobered, "I don't know if I can, Liam. If Brambell found me it would be bad for us all. But I've already decided to pray on the matter. Surely if God can save us, He knows what we need to do to be free of Brambell."

Henry nodded, smiling, "Yes, I believe He will show us."

Henry looked at his friend thoughtfully. He hadn't expected this from Christopher. He knew his friend had been hurting since he had killed the pastor.

"Thank you, Jesus, for showing my friend he's worth saving. Please, show us how to free him from Brambell." Henry prayed as he looked across the morning horizon and the beauty of God's creation.

They docked and Christopher found Mr. Smith to sell his cargo to. When they had made a deal, he went back to the ship and ordered Robert to start unloading the cargo. Then he found Henry on the top deck.

"You can go as soon as I release the men tonight. You'll want to wait until they are gone before you leave. I can't fake your death if they think you just left."

Henry nodded, "What about you?"

"I don't know. God hasn't given me instructions as of yet. You?"

Henry shook his head slowly, "I'm sorry."

Christopher nodded, "It's alright. Hopefully, I'll find a solution someday and I'll come back to see you then."

"Alright, Chris."

"Now get to work," Christopher ordered with a slight smile.

"Yes, sir," Henry grinned and went to help unload the cargo.

Christopher looked around the ship. Everywhere he looked, he saw memories. Unfortunately, they weren't all good, and he wished he could be rid of them. He shook his head to clear it and went to work.

Henry waited until the men had left the ship and then snuck off with his things. He walked quickly towards home. When he saw the lights of the house he broke into a run. He flung open the door and stepped in.

"Mother? Father?" he called out as he dropped his bag on the floor. Footsteps came running from the sitting room and his mother, father, sister, and Lydia stopped short at the sight of him.

He walked over to Lydia and pulled her into his arms tightly.

"I'm so glad you made it safely," he said softly before he leaned down to kiss her.

"Oh, Henry!" his mother's words made him look at her with a smile.

"Hello, mother," he released Lydia and hugged his mother.

Then he looked at his father with a grin, "Father, I have so much to tell you."

His father looked at him with surprise and then nodded

as they shook hands.

Henry turned to Joanna and he read on her face what he knew she was going to ask.

He went over and hugged her as he whispered, "Did you get his letter?"

"What letter? I haven't had one in months. I've been so worried about you both," She whispered back.

Henry wasn't sure what to say, but he knew what Christopher needed to do. No matter how hard.

"I'll tell him you didn't get it. I'm sure he'll explain himself."

"Where is he? Why didn't he come with you?"

"He can't come right now. It's not safe."

She looked at him sternly, "Where is he?"

"Last I know he was headed for the tavern. But I'll make sure he comes tomorrow." Henry said seriously, "I promise."

Joanna didn't say anything else, and he turned his attention back to Lydia.

"I promised to bring you something," he said with a grin.

"And I told you I'd just be happy to have you with me," she said with a smile in return.

Henry reached into his pocket and pulled out the ring. He lifted her hand and put it on her finger.

"Oh, Henry," she said softly. "It's so pretty!"

"I'm not leaving again, Lydia. I'm going to stay with you and we'll buy a farm, just like we talked about. I'll get you your chickens, and we'll plant a big garden full of vegetables." He grinned at her shocked face. "I don't want to leave you again."

"You mean it? You'll stay on land for me?" she asked with hope.

"Yes, I'm staying."

Lydia threw her arms around his neck and tears rolled down her face.

Joanna watched them and she couldn't help but feel sad that Christopher hadn't come to embrace her that way. Would he be staying now that Henry was? She could hardly hope he might.

She couldn't wait until tomorrow to know what was going on.

So as she watched her family go into the sitting room, she snuck to the door and left.

∞∞∞

Christopher sat with Robert, Cale, and Pierre with a mug of ale in front of him that he hadn't touched yet. His mind was on Joanna, and the guilt over Celeste was making him feel frozen. He had to see Joanna and tell her how sorry he was in person. It wasn't fair to let a letter do his talking alone. She deserved better from him.

"Chris!"

He turned sharply to see the very woman he wanted standing before him.

"Joanna." Fear of her being there struck him. He quickly stood and pulled her towards the door. "You can't be here!"

"Chris, please, I need to talk to you."

He pulled her out the door of the tavern and stopped outside.

"It's not safe for you to come here. Why didn't Henry stop you?" The moonlight showed his worried frown.

"He doesn't know I left."

The door to the tavern opened and Christopher stepped protectively closer to Joanna as he watched Stretch and Billy come out. They looked at Christopher and Joanna closely as they passed and moved down the street.

He looked down to find Joanna's hands on his chest and he felt a mixture of longing and guilt. He stepped back and gently took her hands off his chest.

"Didn't you receive my letter?" he asked.

"What letter? I haven't received one since the one you said you were going to France. I've been so worried."

"Joanna, I'll come to you tomorrow and explain. But I

need you to go home. Don't come to the wharf again. It's not safe. There are pirates and I don't trust them to be near you. Please, go home."

Joanna looked at him hurt, and he longed to kiss her hurt away, but he knew he didn't deserve to.

Joanna nodded, "Alright." She reached up to kiss him and he turned his head away, causing her kiss to fall on his cheek. She looked at him with surprise before slowly walking away. He watched until she was at the end of the street and turned off towards her home. Then he went back into the tavern.

∞∞∞

Joanna was confused and hurt as she walked towards home. She didn't understand Christopher's indifference towards her. She was so lost in her thoughts she didn't hear the footsteps coming up to her.

Suddenly strong arms came around her, and a hand clamped over her mouth as she started to scream in fear! Two men held her firmly as they stuck a rag in her mouth. She gagged on the rag and her mouth became drier as she tried to scream. Then one man tried to pick her up but she fought him. He dropped her and she struggled with her skirts to stand and run, but she didn't make it before one of the men grabbed her arm and pulled her back down. Then a hand slapped her hard, and she blacked out.

∞∞∞

Henry opened the tavern door and found Christopher sitting alone at the table. Christopher looked up in surprise as Henry walked in.

"What are you doing here?" he asked Henry.

"I came to find Joanna. She disappeared and I assumed she came to find you."

"She found me and I sent her back home." Christopher rose in worry. "Let's go look for her."

The two men walked the path towards home, looking for Joanna. When they made it to the house, Henry went in to see if she had made it back. When he came back out of the house, he told Christopher she hadn't and they moved back towards the wharf. They stopped at the docks, not knowing where to look next.

"Captain," Robert came towards them quickly, "I just received this note for you. It says Stretch has a woman and he's at your father's house. He will trade her and your father for the ship. He wants to be captain and if you don't let him have it he'll kill them both."

Christopher felt anger well up and he started walking towards his father's house, with Henry and Robert behind him.

∞∞∞

Joanna woke to find herself tied to a chair in a place she'd never been. Her head pounded as she looked around the room and found Mr. Levin sitting tied to a chair as well.

"Ah, she's awake," A man stared at her with an evil grin.

"Who are you?" She asked with a dry throat.

"I'm Stretch, and this is my partner Billy."

"Why are we here?" Mr. Levin asked with a frown.

"I'm ransoming you to the good Captain James. He'll either step down as captain or I'll kill you both."

"He's the captain?" Joanna looked at the man with surprise.

"You mean he didn't write to tell you all about it? Well, let me tell you what your sweetheart has been filling his time with while he's been away."

Stretch proceeded to tell them everything from Christopher killing their Captain Hunter, to Celeste, and the pastor.

"You see I know a lot, and I've been waiting for the perfect opportunity to get back at him for whipping me, and I've finally found it. If he cares about either of you, then he'll relent. And the first thing I'll do as captain is have him whipped."

Joanna stopped listening as she thought about all Christopher had done. The part about Celeste stuck to her the most. Hurt at his indiscretion made her furious with him, and she stared at the floor as angry tears fell from her eyes.

"You're wrong about me," Mr. Levin said, "My son doesn't care about me at all."

"Maybe, but he cares about the girl. I saw him come here the last time we were here, so I asked around and found out you were his father. Then when this pretty little thing came to see him tonight, I realized she was even better leverage."

Suddenly a loud thud on the door came, followed by splintering wood, and the door banged open. Christopher walked in and came towards Stretch with his sword pointed towards the man.

Stretch drew his sword and the two men began to fight. Stretch was sorely outmatched and Christopher ran him through quickly. Then he turned to see Henry had done the same to Billy.

Christopher ran to Joanna and untied her as he knelt in front of her. She was crying and he frowned.

"Did he hurt you?"

Joanna slapped him across the face, "How could you?!"

Christopher stood and stepped back confused, "What do you mean?"

Joanna pointed to Stretch, "He told me about Celeste."

Christopher looked from Joanna to Stretch and then stepped towards her quickly.

"Joanna, I was going to tell you. I'm sorry..."

But she didn't let him finish. She moved away from him,

towards Henry.

"Take me home," she commanded Henry.

Henry looked at Christopher, and Christopher nodded.

He watched them leave with pain in his chest. Then he realized his father was still tied to the chair and he moved to untie him.

"Thank you, son."

"Are you alright?"

"Yes, son."

"Robert, let's get their bodies to the ship. We'll put them overboard when we're back out at sea."

"Yes, sir," Robert picked up Billy's body and started to carry him out.

Christopher looked at his father, "I'll come by tomorrow and help you fix the door."

"Thank you, son."

Christopher nodded and then picked up Stretch's body and carried him to the docks.

Once on the ship, he put Stretch's body in the hold, before going to his cabin and sitting at the desk. Putting his head in his hands, he prayed once again that God would show him the answer.

"Are you alright?" Henry's voice came from the door of the cabin and Christopher looked up.

"How is she?"

"She's angry and upset, but safe."

Christopher nodded, "She has every right. I wish I could have told her myself though. Instead of Stretch rubbing it in her face."

"She'll calm down."

"Even if she does, that doesn't mean much. She'll never have me and I don't blame her."

"What are you going to do, Chris?"

Christopher looked around. "I don't know. But I know I don't want this ship anymore. I would have just given the ship to Stretch if I knew he'd never bring Brambell back to my door."

"Maybe no one should have it," Henry said.

Christopher's eyes widened and he looked at Henry sharply. "That's it! I know what to do!"

He rose quickly and grabbed his bag of money and the bible from his desk. He put them into a bag and proceeded to add a few other things.

"What are you doing?" Henry asked, confused.

"I know our way out." Christopher turned and walked towards the door. "Help me get the ship out of the docks."

Robert came back on the upper deck as they were working to let out the sails enough to blow the ship away from the docks. It was slow going but they managed to get the ship out into open water. Then they proceeded to put the row boats into the water. Once they had the boats down, Christopher dropped his bag into one of the boats before he went back to his cabin and brought out the last two bottles of rum he had.

"Here, dump these everywhere."

Henry looked at him with shock for a moment and then smiled as he took a bottle and started dumping it on everything.

Christopher ran down to the lower deck and grabbed every bottle of rum he could find from the crew. Then went back up and helped Henry and Robert dump every bottle out on the upper deck, top deck, and his cabin. He only saved one bottle.

"Now go get ready to tell the crew to grab their things."

Henry nodded and went to the stairway to the lower deck.

Christopher took a couple of candles and started setting fire to everything in his cabin. Then he moved to the upper deck and once the fire was going he nodded to Henry. Henry and Robert ran down the stairs.

"Get up, the ship is on fire! Abandon ship!" They yelled over and over until every man was up and moving. They all grabbed what they could and ran on deck where they saw the fire raging.

"Everyone to the boats! Abandon ship!" Christopher yelled as he waved the men towards the boats. The men quickly got into the boats and Christopher nodded to Henry to go. They started rowing away from the ship, as Christopher walked up to the top deck and dropped the candles onto the deck. Flames burst up and Christopher stepped back to watch. Then he took the last bottle of rum out.

"Goodbye, you temptress, Maria."

He tossed the bottle into the fire where it exploded into more flames that licked at the deck. He watched a moment more until he was sure the fire was blazing and he backed away as it slowly came towards him.

Then he stepped up onto the side of the ship. With one look back he turned away and dove into the water.

He swam to shore where he found the rest of the crew standing on the dock watching their ship go up in flames. He climbed up onto the dock and stood next to Henry to watch a moment before taking his bag from the rowboat and turning to his crew.

"The Maria's gone. You're all free to go wherever you wish. May the winds be with you."

With that, he nodded to Henry and they both walked away without looking back.

Chapter 16

Christopher walked towards the house nervously. He wasn't sure what he'd say, but he prayed for the right words as he walked. He stopped at the door and paused for a moment before he knocked. The door opened to Mrs. Johnson who looked at him happily. Then she hugged him tightly.

"Come in, dear. Let me get you some breakfast."

"I just came to see Joanna and the pastor."

"Well the pastor isn't finished with his morning prayers yet, but Joanna is in the kitchen."

He followed her into the kitchen and saw Joanna standing by the fireplace, stirring something in the pot.

"Joanna," he said softly.

She looked up at him with surprise and then anger came to her face. "What are you doing here?"

"I came to tell you something if you'll hear me."

She stared at him a moment more before setting down the spoon and walking over to him.

"Can we go outside?"

She nodded curtly and led the way outside, where she stopped and turned to him with her arms crossed over her chest. Then suddenly she noticed something in the distance that brought a frown to her lovely face.

"There's smoke over there. What could be on fire?"

He didn't look toward the smoke, he just looked at her seriously.

"It's my ship."

She looked at him with surprise, "Your ship is gone?"

"Yes, I burnt it last night."

She looked at him with shock now.

"It's what I've come to tell you. I've decided I don't want that life anymore. I want to live a life that God guides me to. I regret everything I've done. I especially never meant to hurt you, Joanna. It will always fill me with grief to know I brought you so much pain. I understand if you can't, but I hope someday you'll forgive me. I'm truly sorry. I can't undo what's been done though, and I have to move on to whatever life God has for me."

She stared at the ground and he saw a tear fall down her cheek.

Suddenly the door opened and the pastor stepped out.

"Mrs. Johnson said you wanted to speak to me?" he said as he walked over to Christopher and stood protectively near Joanna. Christopher turned to look the man in the eyes.

"Yes, sir. I will be giving up my life as a sailor and I want to make a new life for myself. But there's something I'd like to do first."

"What's that?" The older man looked skeptical.

"I'd like to ask if you would baptize me before I leave."

A small gasp came from Joanna, but he didn't look at her. He just stared at the pastor.

"You want to live a life for the Lord?" The pastor looked surprised and thoughtful.

"Yes, sir."

"Henry has expressed the same desire." He studied Christopher a moment before nodding, "I'll be glad to do so this Sabbath."

Christopher smiled slightly and stuck out his hand. "Thank you, sir. I'll be there early Sabbath morning for services."

"Good." The pastor turned to walk away, but turned back, "Christopher, only a strong man would submit to God. I'm proud of you, son."

Christopher smiled, "Thank you, sir."

The pastor walked back into the house and closed the door.

Christopher looked at Joanna then, and nodded, "Good

day, Joanna."

Joanna watched him walk away and she felt like her heart was walking away with him. Was he worth forgiving? He was taking steps to be with God. If God can forgive him, then there was no reason she shouldn't. But what did forgiving him mean? Could she still love him after what he'd done? Could she live without him? When he'd turned down the street out of sight, she turned and walked back into the house. She spent the rest of the day thinking about her questions.

∞∞∞

Christopher held the door while his father hammered the new hinges onto the doorpost.

"Alright, that's the last one," his father said as he stood back up.

Christopher let go and swung the door closed.

"Would you like some tea, son?"

"Yes, thank you," Christopher followed him into the kitchen and sat down at the table.

"I've got some cookies that the lady down the street made. She's been kind enough to look out for me since you've been away. I met her at church on my first Sabbath, and we've been friends since. Her poor husband passed away a couple of years ago from an illness."

His father set a plate of cookies on the table and then poured hot water into cups with tea leaves. Then he sat down at the table with Christopher.

"Father, you once asked me if I could forgive you. At the time I thought I could never forgive you for all that you did to me. Then I became a pirate and did things that I'm not proud of. I regret them and wish I could take them back. I asked others to forgive me, but I knew I didn't deserve it. But I found God and I know He's forgiven me. Even if others don't, I take comfort in knowing He has. I guess what I'm trying to say is that I think I understand what you feel. And I want you to know that I do forgive you."

His father smiled and tears came to his eyes, "Thank you, son."

"I'd also like to ask if you'd come to my baptism on Sabbath?"

"I'd be honored to, son."

Christopher nodded and then took a sip of the tea.

"When do you leave?" his father asked.

"I don't know. I won't be sailing anymore, but I don't know what I'll be doing now. I don't think I can stay here though."

"Because of Miss Johnson?"

Christopher nodded sadly.

"Whatever you do, let me know where you're going. Maybe I can come see you."

"I will."

"Where are you staying if you're leaving the ship?"

"I'm staying at the tavern for now."

"Why don't you stay here, son? No need to waste your money there."

"Are you sure?"

"Of course. It'd be nice to have you here, even for a short time."

Christopher smiled, "Thank you. I'll go get my things and bring them back."

"While you do that, I'll fix us some dinner."

Christopher nodded and rose to leave as his father smiled brightly.

Sabbath morning, Christopher and his father walked to

the church and sat in the back. It was the first service that Christopher remembered truly listening to. By the end of the sermon, he felt a renewed sense of love towards God, for having saved him from a life full of pain. Pastor Johnson invited the church family to the baptisms, and the church group made their way down to a secluded beach where he proceeded to baptize Henry and Christopher.

When they were coming back out of the water, Christopher felt different. He felt like he had shed off his old self, to make way for a new person. He truly felt the gift of freedom he'd been given. The freedom to live a new life, full of God's love and grace.

The group started to disperse until only his father and the Johnsons were left.

"We'd like to invite you both to dinner if you'd like to come."

The pastor's invitation came as a surprise to Christopher. He had never been welcomed to their home by the pastor himself.

Christopher smiled slightly, "Thank you, sir, but I have to be going."

"Where are you going?" Mrs. Johnson asked with confusion.

Christopher wasn't sure what to tell her. He shook his head.

"I don't know yet. I'm thinking I'll go to the south. Maybe to Charleston."

"What could you possibly do in Charleston that you can't do here?" Mrs. Johnson asked with tears coming to her eyes. "We just got you back, and now you're leaving again. I thought you'd stay."

"I'm sorry, you've all been very kind to me, and I appreciate everything you've done."

He went to the pastor and shook his hand. Then he went to Mrs. Johnson and hugged her. He stopped when he came to Henry.

"You promised to come home once in a while to see me." Henry looked at him sternly. "Wouldn't hurt to write too."

Christopher nodded before he hugged Henry, "I love you, brother."

"Take care, Chris."

The men parted and Joanna's face came into view. He wasn't sure what to say to her so he just smiled a little before turning away and walking back up the path from the beach with his father.

He was standing on top of the small hill that overlooked the beach when he heard Joanna yell.

"Chris, wait!"

He turned to see her hurry up the hill behind him and then stopped in front of him.

"I just needed to say something."

He looked at her and nodded seriously. He braced himself for what might come.

"I wanted you to know that I forgive you."

He looked at her with surprise, "You do?"

She nodded.

"Thank you, Joanna. That means a lot to me."

"I've also been thinking about something else."

"Oh?"

She bit her lip and he waited patiently.

Suddenly she reached up and took his head in her hands, and kissed him sweetly. When she released him, he felt an overwhelming love for her, but also, confusion.

"Joanna?"

"I love you, Christopher Levin. I don't want you to go. I want you to stay with me forever."

A grin spread across his face, "Are you asking me to marry you, Joanna Johnson?"

"Yes, I guess I am," she said as she stuck her nose up a little.

He suddenly put his arms around her and picked her up, swinging her around. Then he put her down and grabbed her face in his gentle hands.

"I love you, Joanna. I'd happily stay here with you forever."

She smiled up at him happily, before he leaned down to kiss her.

Epilogue

"As we lay Pastor Johnson to rest this day, we can be assured that he is sleeping peacefully, waiting for our Savior to return." Christopher looked over the congregation that was now his alone to lead. The weight of responsibility weighed heavily on him, but it was a weight he was glad to bear. "Please remember our family in your prayers today, thank you."

The congregation broke up and he watched them go as the words of the pastor came to his mind.

"Lead them with strength and compassion. More compassion than I showed you, son."

Christopher smiled slightly as he remembered the man who had become a friend, not just a father-in-law. He had instructed and led Christopher to a life in the church. Christopher looked over at Joanna and smiled as she looked at him with tears in her eyes.

"First Mother and now Father. What will we ever do without them?" she said softly.

He embraced her, "We'll carry on the way they would have. Showing love to everyone we meet. Come, let's see if Henry and Lydia want to join us for supper before they head back to the farm."

Joanna nodded and they turned to walk towards Henry and Lydia.

"Father, may George and I go to the river?" his son Grant asked as he ran up.

"Let's ask your uncle first," Christopher said as he ruffled his son's black hair.

"I want to go to the river too." Violet's pouty violet eyes

appeared from behind her mother.

"No! You can't come, you're a girl," Grant said with a frown.

"Really now, Grant," Joanna rolled her eyes.

"Son, that wasn't the way to say that you didn't want Violet to come. You should have said, 'We'd like to go alone, please.'" Christopher looked at his son sternly, "Now please apologize to your sister for being rude."

"I'm sorry," Grant said half-heartedly.

"The boys want to go to the river," Christopher said to Henry as they walked up.

Henry nodded soberly.

"How about we let them play and the rest of us will go to the house for supper?"

"That sounds fine, Chris," Henry nodded to his redheaded son, "Be back soon. We have to get home."

"Yes, sir."

And with that, the boys were off running. They ran to their secret spot by the river and pulled out their sticks. Then the sword fight began.

Afterword

If you are feeling called by God to live your life in His service, seek counsil of a friend or family member you trust who can guide you and answer questions you have. If you don't currently have such a person, thats alright, because your great Creator who adores you, awaits your prayers! Pray and ask His forgiveness. Seek His involvement in your life. Then open His precious word and start reading! The beginning is the best place to start!

The Lord bless thee, and keep thee:
The Lord make his face shine upon thee, and be gracious unto thee:
The Lord lift up his countenance upon thee, and give thee peace.
Numbers 6:24-26

Acknowledgements

My thanks to my editor and friend Craig Moore for all your support and help! I could never have made it this far with my work without your support and great ideas! And to Melanie for supporting our long hours of "work"! Thank you for letting me commandeer your husband to talk writing! I love you both so much! Thank you for being my support!

I would also like to thank Brian Hall for the beautiful cover! I highly recommend him to other author's looking for a cover design.
providentialstudios.com

About The Author

Ann S. Mooney

As a homemaker and homeschooling mom of four kids, Ann happily follows her soldier around the country from post to post. Their family see's the military life as one of adventure where they meet incredible people in each place they move. Earning a Bachelors degree in clinical psychology brought a new career to mind and she is working on a Masters in Human Services, trauma and crisis couseling. Her love of writing will always be her favorite creative outlet. Each story comes from her heart and dreams, and each charactor is a piece of who she is inside.

Made in the USA
Coppell, TX
13 May 2024